Lucy Monroe

THE SHEIKH'S BARTERED BRIDE

Surrender To
The Sheikh

HARLEQUIN®

TORONTO • NEW YORK • LONDON
AMSTERDAM • PARIS • SYDNEY • HAMBURG
STOCKHOLM • ATHENS • TOKYO • MILAN • MADRID
PRAGUE • WARSAW • BUDAPEST • AUCKLAND

To Isabelle...You are more precious to me than words
can ever express and I thank God daily for giving you
to me as a very special gift. With love, Lucy

ISBN 0-373-12447-3

THE SHEIKH'S BARTERED BRIDE

First North American Publication 2005.

Copyright © 2004 by Lucy Monroe.

www.eHarlequin.com

Printed in U.S.A.

CHAPTER ONE

"MISS BENNING."

She wasn't Miss Benning. She was Catherine Marie, captive of The Hawk, a sheikh who still lived by the code of the desert, where only the strongest survived.

He was coming now. She could hear his deep, masculine voice as he spoke in a tongue she did not understand to someone outside her tent. She struggled against the cords that bound her hands, but it was useless. The silk scarves were soft, but strong and she could not get her hands free.

If she did, what would she do? Run?

Where?

She was in the middle of the desert. The sun beat against the tent, heating up the cavernous interior. She wouldn't last a day in the vast wasteland on her own.

Then he was there, standing in the entrance to the room in which she was held. His features were cast in shadow. All she could see was his big body encased in the white pants and tunic typical of his people. A black robe, his *abaya*, fell from his massive shoulders to mid-calf and his head was covered with the red and white *smagh* that denoted his position as sheikh. The headband holding it in place was made of twisted black leather.

He was less than fifteen feet away, but still his face was hidden from her by the shadows. Only the strong line of his jaw denoting his arrogance was discernable.

"Miss Benning!"

Catherine Marie Benning's head snapped up from where it had been resting against her fist and her eyes slowly focused on her surroundings. Tent walls hung with faded silks, to be replaced by cool gray cement, relieved only by the posters advertising the upcoming book drive and literacy event. They were the walls of the break room in the Whitehaven Public Library, much closer to a cold and wet Seattle, Washington than the blistering hot deserts of the Sahara.

Fluorescent light cast a harsh glow over the pointed features of the woman standing in front of her.

"Yes, Mrs. Camden?"

Straightening her double-knit polyester blazer, almost identical in color to the library's walls, Mrs. Camden, Catherine's superior, sniffed. "Your head was off in the clouds again, Miss Benning."

The disapproval in the older woman's voice grated against Catherine's usually limitless patience. Perhaps if the man in her fantasies would ever show his face, she wouldn't be feeling so frustrated, but he did not. This time had been no different. The Hawk was as elusive to her imagination as he was in it.

"I'm still on break," she gently reminded the older woman.

"Yes, well, we all do what we must."

Recognizing the beginnings of a familiar lecture, Catherine stifled a sigh at the knowledge her lunch break was to be cut short. Again.

Hakim bin Omar al Kadar walked into the library and scanned the reference area for sight of Catherine Marie Benning. Her picture was indelibly printed on his mind. His future wife. While arranged marriages were not uncommon in the royal family of Jawhar, his was unique.

Catherine Marie Benning was unaware that she was to become his wife. Her father wanted it that way.

One of the stipulations of the deal between Hakim's uncle and Harold Benning was that Hakim convince Catherine to become his wife without telling her about the arrangement between her father and the King of Jawhar. Hakim had not asked why. Having been educated in the West, Hakim knew that American women did not view arranged marriages with the same equanimity the women of his family did.

He would have to court Catherine, but that would be no hardship. Even in an arranged marriage, a royal prince of Jawhar was expected to court his intended bride. This marriage would be no different. He would give her a month.

Ten weeks ago, his uncle had been apprised by Harold Benning of the probable deposits of a rare mineral in the mountains of Jawhar. The American had suggested a partnership between Benning Excavations and the royal family of Jawhar.

The two men had still been negotiating terms when Hakim had been attacked while out riding in the desert in the early hours of the morning. Investigations had revealed that the assassination attempt had been made by the same group of dissidents responsible for his parents' deaths twenty years before.

Hakim was unclear how marriage for Catherine had become part of the deal. He knew only that his uncle considered it convenient. Should the need for long-term living visas arise for the royal family, Hakim would be in a position to sponsor them as the spouse of an American. There would be no need to go through regular diplomatic channels, thus preserving the privacy and pride of his family.

The royal family of Jawhar had not sought political asylum from another country in the three centuries of its reign and they never would. Already overseeing the family's interests in America, Hakim had been the logical choice for the alliance.

Harold Benning also saw the marriage as beneficial. His concern over the continued single state of his twenty-four-year old daughter had been obvious. According to him, she never even dated.

The result of the older men's negations had been a Royal Decree: Hakim was to marry Catherine Benning.

He spotted his quarry helping a small boy on the other side of the room. She stretched to pull a book from the shelf and the button-up black sweater she wore above a long, straight skirt caught his attention. Molding her breasts, it revealed a surprisingly lush feminine form and he felt himself stir.

This was unexpected. Her picture had revealed a pretty woman, but nothing like the exotic beauties he had bedded in the past. That he should react so readily to such an innocent sight made him stop in his journey toward her.

What had so aroused him? Her skin was pale, but not alabaster. Her hair was blond, but a dark blond and twisted up on the back of her head as it was, it looked drab. Her eyes were a shock, a gentian-blue that had startled him with their intensity in the picture and were even more unusual in person.

Aside from the eyes, nothing about her stood out and yet his body's response could not be denied. He wanted her. While he had experienced this sort of instant physical attraction before, it had been with a lot more provocation. A certain way of walking, dressing or an alluring look. Catherine Benning exhibited none of these.

It was a puzzling, but not unpleasant surprise. A genuine physical attraction on his part would make the job of her seduction that much easier. He had been prepared to do his duty regardless of personal attraction. Country came first. Family came second. His own needs and desires last of all.

He walked forward, stopping a little to her left. As the boy walked away, her dark sapphire gaze did a quick survey of the room, skimming over him, and then settled back on a man who had come to stand in front of the desk.

But even as she pointed to something on her computer monitor, her gaze flicked back to Hakim. And stayed. He met her eyes, noting peripherally the man she had been helping walk away. The next person in line went unnoticed as her attention remained on him.

She appeared poleaxed and he smiled.

Her entire body went taut and her cheeks pinkened, but she did not look away.

His smile went up a notch. Fulfilling his duty would be a simple matter of turning that attraction into a desire to wed.

"Miss Benning! Pay attention. You have patrons to serve."

The martinet haranguing Catherine was no doubt the dragon of a boss Harold Benning had mentioned when briefing Hakim on his daughter.

Catherine's head snapped around and her blush intensified, but she did not stammer as she answered the older woman. "I'm sorry. My mind wandered." She turned to the next person in line, repeated her apology and asked how she could help them, effectively dismissing her superior.

The older woman harrumphed and marched away like a petty general deprived of his battle spoils.

He waited until the last of the line had walked away before greeting Catherine. "Good afternoon."

She smiled, her eyes even more startling up close. The blush was back. "Hi. What can I do for you?"

"I am interested in antique telescopes and the history of stargazing. Perhaps you can direct me to a good reference."

Her eyes lit with interest. "Is this a new hobby for you?"

"Fairly new." As recent as the discussion Hakim had had with her father. Although Hakim's own father had shared Catherine's passionate interest in ancient stargazing, since his death, his books had remained unused in the observatory in the Kadar Palace.

"It's one of my personal interests. If you've got a few minutes I'll show you the right section and point out a few books that I think are particularly good."

"I would like that very much."

Catherine sucked in air, trying to calm her racing heart as she led the handsome and rather imposing man to the proper nonfiction area of her library. The aura of barely leashed power surrounding him was enough to send her pulse rocketing, but the fact that he physically embodied every characteristic of her ideal fantasy tipped her senses into dangerous territory.

At least a couple of inches over six feet, his muscle-honed body towered above her own five foot seven in a way that made her feel small beside him. Even knowing she was not. The silky black hair on his head was only a shade darker than the color of his eyes and if he didn't speak with such impeccable English, she would think he was the sheikh of her fantasies.

A wave of totally unfamiliar desire swept over her, leaving her even more breathless and confused.

He hadn't touched her and somehow she had always believed this level of sexual awareness could only accompany touch. She'd been wrong.

They stopped in front of a row of books. She pulled one off the shelf and handed it to him. "This is my favorite. I have my own first-edition copy at home."

He took the book and his fingers briefly brushed hers. She jumped back, shocked by the contact. Her body throbbed in a way she hadn't experienced before, but she desperately tried to look unaffected by his nearness.

"I am sorry." His black gaze probed her own, leaving her even more unsettled.

She shook her head, but could feel that infernal blush crawling along her skin again. "It's nothing." Less than nothing. Or at least it should have been.

He flipped open the book and looked at it. She knew she should go, but she couldn't make her legs move in the direction of the reference desk.

The book shut with a snap and his dark gaze settled on her again. "Do you recommend anything else?"

"Yes." She spent another ten minutes pointing out different books and suggesting a couple of periodicals he might be interested in ordering.

"Thank you very much, Miss…"

"Benning, but please call me Catherine."

"I am Hakim."

"That's an Arabic name."

His mouth twitched. "Yes."

"But your English is perfect." What an inane thing

to say. Lots of Arabic people lived in the Seattle area, many of them second or third generation Americans.

"So it should be," he drawled in a voice programmed to melt her insides. "The royal tutor would be most displeased if one of his pupils should speak with anything less than complete mastery."

"Royal?" The word came out sounding choked.

"Forgive me. I am Hakim bin Omar al Kadar, prince in the royal family of Jawhar."

She was breathing, but her lungs felt starved of oxygen. A prince? She'd been talking to a prince for more than ten minutes. Lusting after him! Heavens. Her half-formed idea of inviting him to attend the next meeting of the Antique Telescope Society died a swift death. Unfortunately the attraction he held for her did not.

She swallowed. "Can I help you with anything else?"

"I have taken up enough of your time."

"There's a society for people interested in antique telescopes in Seattle," she found herself blurting out, unable to let it go at that. She wouldn't invite him to meet her there, but she could tell him about the meeting.

"Yes?"

"They meet tonight." She named the time and place.

"Will I see you there?" he asked.

"Probably not." She would be there, but she sat in the back of the room and he was not the sort of man content to enjoy anything from the sidelines.

She wasn't wholly content, either, but she didn't know how to break a lifetime of conditioning.

"You will not attend?" He actually looked disappointed.

"I always go."

"Then I shall see you."

She shrugged. "It's a big group."

"I will look for you, Catherine."

She barely stopped herself from blurting out the question, "Why?" Instead she smiled. "Then maybe we *will* run into each other."

"I do not leave such matters to fate."

No doubt. He was much too decisive. "Until tonight then."

She turned to go and was only marginally disappointed he did not call her back. After all, he'd said he would look for her.

He checked the books out she had recommended and left the library a few minutes later.

Catherine watched him go, certain of one thing. The sheikh of her fantasies would no longer be faceless.

He would have the features of Hakim.

CHAPTER TWO

CATHERINE walked into the meeting room in one of Seattle's posh downtown hotels. Though she was early, over half of the seats were already taken. She scanned the crowd for Hakim while butterflies with hobnail boots danced an Irish jig on the inside of her stomach.

Would he be here?

Would he really be looking for her?

It was hard to believe. Even harder to accept the sensations she felt at the mere thought of his presence.

A scar-riddled face and subsequent laser treatments had meant she'd missed out on dating in both high school and college. Her shyness had been so ingrained by then that the *late blooming* her parents had expected never materialized. She thought she'd come to terms with the fact she would most likely die a maiden aunt in the best tradition of little old ladies with white hair and homes filled with other people's memories. She was too shy to pursue men and too ordinary to be pursued. Yet something about Hakim compelled her to step outside her comfort zone.

And that scared her.

No way would a guy like that return her interest.

"Catherine. You have arrived."

She knew the owner of the deeply masculine voice, even as she turned. "Good evening, Hakim."

"Will you sit with me?"

She nodded, unable to immediately voice her acceptance.

He led her to a chair in the middle of the room, much closer to the front than she usually sat. Taking her arm, he helped her into the seat with a courtesy that was both captivating and alarming. Alarming because it meant he touched her and the feel of his warm fingers on her arm was enough to send her senses reeling.

Several pairs of eyes turned to watch them take their seats, the curiosity of the onlookers palpable. She smiled slightly at an elderly woman whose stare was filled with avid interest. Catherine remembered talking to her at the last meeting. She was nice, but a bit nosy.

Catherine moved her own gaze to the front of the room where tonight's speaker stood talking to the president of the society.

The speaker was the leading authority on George Lee and Sons telescopes. He was supposed to bring along one from his collection for the society members to look at up close. She couldn't wait to see it and thought the red silk covered shape in the front of the room must be it.

She was proved right forty minutes later when the silk cover was removed and the general assembly was invited to come forward and take a look.

"You wish to see it?" Hakim asked her.

She shrugged.

"What does this shrug mean?"

She turned her head, allowing herself the luxury of a full-on look. The impact was that of a bomb exploding in her brain and she almost gasped, but held back the revealing sound.

She smiled wryly, knowing herself. "The shrug means I'll probably forego the pleasure."

"I will accompany you."

Like a security blanket? "It's not that," she denied,

even though it was exactly that. "I'd just rather not wait in line. Do you see how many people are already waiting to look at it?"

Hakim looked toward the line of society members and then back at her. "Are you quite certain you do not wish to see it?"

Even a George Lee and Sons telescope could not compete with Hakim for her interest, she admitted to herself. "Very sure."

"Then, perhaps you would consent to dinner with me this evening and we could discuss my new hobby. You appear highly knowledgeable in the subject."

"Dinner?" she parroted.

"Are you concerned about sharing a meal with a stranger?"

The quite justifiable concern had never entered her mind, but then she'd never been in a sheikh's company before, nor had she ever experienced the debilitating cocktail of feelings being near him elicited in her body.

"No," she said, shocking herself and making his eyes widen fractionally.

"Then you will allow me to buy you dinner this evening?"

"I don't know..."

"Please." The word sounded much more like a command than any sort of pleading, yet it affected her just the same.

"I suppose I could follow you to the restaurant in my car." She should show at least a rudimentary level of self-protection.

"Very well. Is seafood to your liking?"

Her mouth watered at the thought. "I adore it."

"There is a beautiful restaurant not a block from here. We could walk."

"I think it's just starting to rain," she said.

His lips tilted in a sardonic smile. "If so, I will lend you my raincoat."

She laughed at the instant picture she had of herself in a raincoat several sizes too big. "That won't be necessary. I just thought you probably wouldn't like to walk if it was wet out."

"I would not have suggested it otherwise."

"Of course."

It was a short walk and though the gray clouds were heavy with moisture, it did not rain.

They spent dinner discussing her favorite hobby. She was surprised at his knowledge and said so.

"I read the books you gave me this afternoon."

"Already?"

It was his turn to shrug. "Most of them."

"Wow. I guess you didn't have to go back to work."

"We all must have our priorities," he said with a smile.

"I wouldn't have pegged you as someone who put his hobbies above his work."

"There are times when the unexpected takes precedence in our lives."

She wondered at the mysterious statement, but did not know him well enough to ask about it.

They both declined dessert and he walked her back to her car. He took her keys from her and unlocked it. Opening the door, he indicated she should get inside.

She stopped before bending down to get into the driver's seat. "Thank you for dinner."

"It was my pleasure, Catherine."

Two days later, Hakim invited her to attend a Saturday showing of a journey among the stars at the theater. It required spending the whole day together as well as a three-hour drive to Portland. The prospect of all that time with just her and Hakim in the enclosed space of a car had her nerves completely on edge. She jumped when the security buzzer rang to announce his arrival.

She pressed the button on the small black communications box. "I'll be right down."

"I'll be waiting." His short reply came; his voice even sounded exotic and sexy over the apartment building's tinny intercom system. She was still finding it difficult to believe that such a gorgeous man had a serious interest in her. Grabbing her hold-all and purse, she left the apartment.

When she got downstairs, she found him waiting in the lobby.

"Good morning, Catherine. Are you ready to go?"

She nodded, while her eyes devoured the sight of him. Wearing a snug-fitting black sweater and tan trousers that managed to emphasize his well-developed muscles, he made her mouth go dry with desire.

She licked her lips and swallowed. "I've got everything I need."

"Then, let's go." He took her arm and led her outside where a long, black limousine waited.

"I thought you were driving."

"I wanted to be able to focus my attention on you. There is a privacy window. We will be as secluded as we desire."

The way he said it made totally inappropriate images swirl through her head and her nipples tightened almost painfully. It was such an unexpected sensation, she gasped.

"Are you well?"

"F-fine," she stuttered before practically diving into the backseat of the limousine.

As a tactic to hide her discomposure from him, it was no doubt a dismal failure. Most of his escorts probably waited for him to help them into the car. Of course, these same escorts most likely had a love life outside of their fantasies and could handle the close proximity of such a sexy man with equanimity.

Not so her.

She was in over her head and the man had never even kissed her. When he took the seat opposite her, her breasts swelled at his nearness.

And his smile was positively lethal to her self-control.

"Would you like some refreshments?" He flipped open a small door in the side console of the car to reveal a fully stocked fridge.

"Some juice would be nice." She was really proud of herself when her voice came out fairly normal.

He poured her a glass of cranberry juice and handed it to her. "So, are antique telescopes your only hobby?"

"Oh, no. I'm an avid reader. I guess that makes sense, me working in a library."

"I think I expected that, yes."

She returned the droll smile. "Right, but I also love hiking nature trails."

His brows rose at that and she couldn't help a rueful shrug of acknowledgment to his surprise.

"Maybe I should have said ambling through the woods."

"Ah." He sipped at his mineral water. "And do you daydream as you walk, I wonder."

She could not hide her own surprise that he had guessed something so private about her quite accurately.

"Yes. Being outside and away from people is sort of magical."

"I too like the outdoors, but prefer the desert to the woods."

"Please tell me about it."

And he did, but he deftly directed the conversation back to her on several occasions and they spent the long drive talking about subjects she rarely discussed with anyone but her sister. Hakim seemed to understand her shyness and was not bothered by it, which made it easier for her to be open with him.

He also never dismissed her views as her father was so adept at doing. Hakim listened and as he listened, Catherine found herself falling under the spell of his personality.

He took her to lunch at a restaurant that overlooked the Willamette River. The food was superb, the view of the river amazing and his company overwhelming to her heart and her senses. She was very much afraid that she was falling deeply and irrevocably in love with a man that was far out of her league.

When they'd settled into their seats at the theater, Hakim slipped his arm over Catherine's shoulders, smiling to himself when she stiffened, but did not pull away. She was not used to a man's touch, but her body gave all the signals of being ready for a sexual awakening. The latent and untapped passion he sensed in her would play to his advantage, making it easy for him to seduce her into marriage and fulfill his duty.

His specialized training had made it possible to save himself from the recent assassination attempt, but his parents had not been so lucky. He had been unable to save them and the knowledge still haunted him.

The fact that he had been ten years old at the time did nothing to assuage his need to protect his family now, whatever the cost.

He could still remember the sound of his mother's scream as she watched her husband shot before her eyes, a scream cut short by another gunshot. His little sister had whimpered beside him and he'd taken her hand, leading her out of the palace via the secret passage known only to members of the royal family and their most trusted servants.

Days of grueling heat in the desert sun had followed as Hakim had used the knowledge taught him by his Bedouin grandfather to seek shelter in the wild for him and his small sister. He had eventually found his grandfather's tribe. He and his sister had survived, but Hakim would never forget the cost.

A small sound from Catherine brought him back to the present. He realized he had been caressing her neck with his thumb. Her eyes were fixed on the huge screen, but her body was wholly attuned to him and hummed with sexual excitement.

A month of seducing her toward marriage might very well be overkill.

Catherine reveled in the feel of Hakim's arms around her and pretended it meant more than it did. It was only natural that he ask her to dance with him. After all, he was her escort for the evening and everyone else was dancing.

The black-tie charity ball was to raise money for St. Jude's Children's Hospital. She'd invited Hakim to be her escort, half expecting him to say no, but he hadn't. He'd agreed to bring her and even to have dinner with her family beforehand.

Her mother and sister were completely charmed by his exotic charisma and enigmatic presence. Even in a business suit and tie, the man exuded sheikhness.

"Your sister is very kind."

She let her body move infinitesimally closer to his and fought the urge to lay her head on his shoulder and just breathe in his essence. "Yes. She and I are very close."

"This is good."

"I think so." She smiled up at him.

His expression remained serious. "Family is very important."

"Yes, it is."

She wasn't sure where this was headed.

"Having children, passing one's heritage from one generation to the next is also important."

"I agree. I can't imagine a married couple not wanting children."

Finally he smiled. "Perhaps there are those that have their reasons, but you would never be one of them."

She thought longingly of marriage and family, specifically with this man and it was all she could do to keep her smile pasted in place. "No, I'd never be one of them."

She was unlikely ever to be married at all, but why bring up that depressing thought?

His thumb started a caressing rotation in the small of her back and her thoughts scattered, even the depressing ones.

Closing her eyes, she gave into the urge to let her cheek rest against his chest. He'd probably never ask her to dance again, but she just couldn't help herself.

Instead of acting offended by her forwardness, Hakim

settled her more fully against him and danced with her until the music changed to a faster beat.

He didn't ask her to dance again that evening, but he didn't neglect her, either. Using his easy sophistication to deflect the interest of other women who approached them with the intention of flirting with him, he kept his interest fixed firmly on her and her heart gave up the battle.

She was in love.

Hopelessly.

Helplessly.

Completely.

Catherine opened the card attached to the flowers. It read, "For a woman whose inner beauty blooms with more loveliness than a rose."

Tears filled her eyes and it was all she could do not to cry. She and Hakim had spent the night before at a benefit concert. Catherine had gotten up and spoken on behalf of the children and their hopes and dreams. She'd been shaking with nerves, but she'd felt compelled to make a plea on the foundation's behalf.

Afterward, Hakim had told her that her obvious love of children and compassion for them had shown through even her nervousness. She'd been warmed by the compliment, but the long-stemmed red roses totally overwhelmed her.

She put the vase on the corner of her desk where both she and the rest of the librarians could see them easily.

Picking up a pile of papers that needed filing, she contemplated the crimson blooms. He made her feel so special, even if they were just friends. Sometimes it felt like more than friendship and her hopes would soar, but what else could it be when he never so much as kiss-ed her?

They spent a lot of time together and her attraction for him grew with each occasion, but he appeared un-affected on a physical level by her.

She wasn't surprised.

She was hardly the type to inspire unbridled lust in a man like Hakim, but her desire for him continued unabated. Growing with each successive meeting, both it and the desire to be in his company became gnawing needs within her.

Her thoughts stilled along with the rest of her as Hakim walked into the library. She should be used to his arrival by now, it happened often enough and every time since the first, he'd made it clear he had come specifically to see her.

He walked toward her with an unconscious arrogance that she found rather endearing. He was just so sure of himself, but then he was rich, gorgeous and had been raised a prince. Why wouldn't he be?

She remembered the papers in her hand just as he reached her desk and leaned over to put them away quickly.

Hakim stopped in front of Catherine's desk, just as she bent to put something away in the lowest drawer.

"Catherine…"

Her body straightened and her intense blue gaze met with his, her mouth twisted in a rueful grimace. "Sorry, I just remembered I had to file these—" she waved a sheaf of papers in her hand "—when I saw you."

"And it could not wait until you had greeted me?" he asked with some amusement.

"I might have forgotten easily."

Did she realize what she was giving away with that admission? He already knew he had a definite impact on her ability to concentrate, but a more sophisticated woman would not have admitted it.

"Then I shall have to content myself conversing with the top of your head while you finish."

"Sometimes, you sound so formal. Is that because the Arabic language is a more formal language, or is it because English is your second language and therefore you don't slip into slang as easily?"

Not for the first time, her rapid change in topic left him slightly disorientated. "French is my second language," he said in answer to her question, "I did not learn English until I had mastered it."

She tilted her head to one side. "Oh. I've always thought French would be a lovely language to learn. I studied German and Spanish in school, but I have to admit I don't have a facility for it."

"I did not come to discuss my fluency in other languages."

"Of course you didn't." She smiled. "Why did you come?"

"To see my friend."

Something flickered in her eyes at the word "friend", but was gone too quickly for him to interpret.

"Oh," she said again. "How many are you?"

"How many what, little kitten?"

Her face heated to rose red as he knew it would at the small endearment. Such words were common in his culture between a man and the woman he intended to marry. They were nothing more than an admission of his intent, but they flustered Catherine a great deal.

"How many languages are you fluent in?" Her voice

was breathless and he had the not so shocking urge to steal her breath completely with a kiss.

He could not do it of course. Not here and not yet, but soon. He smiled in anticipation, causing her eyes to widen.

"I'm fluent in French, English, Arabic and all the dialects of my people, little kitten." He repeated the phrase on purpose just to watch the effect it had on her, which was perhaps unfair of him.

It was startling. She sucked in air, grimaced and then whispered, "Hardly little."

While she was maybe an inch above average in height for a woman, she often made comments as if she saw herself as some kind of Amazon. He stepped toward her until he stood only a few inches from her and reached out to brush the smooth curve of her neck with one fingertip. "To me, very little."

She trembled and he smiled.

Very soon she would be his.

Her head tilted back and she eyed his six-foot two-inch frame with unmistakable longing. "I suppose so."

He wanted to kiss her. It took every bit of the self-discipline developed in his training with the elite guard to step back and drop his hand.

"I came to see if you would like to join me for dinner tonight."

Her mouth opened and closed with no sound issuing forth. They had known each other for three weeks now and eaten numerous meals together, as well as attending several formal functions. Yet she acted shocked every time he asked her out.

"Come, this is not such a surprise. We had lunch together only yesterday."

She smiled whimsically. "That's why I'm surprised. I thought you'd want to spend time with…"

Her voice trailed off, but her eyes told him what she had been about to say. *Other women.* She had so little concept of her own value. While he should be relieved his duty would be so easy to see through, it made him angry she dismissed herself so easily.

"I want to spend time with no other woman."

He had no difficulty reading her expression now. Her eyes were filled with both joy and hope. Yes. She was ready. He had courted her long enough.

"I would love to have dinner with you."

"Then I shall see you this evening." He turned to go.

"Hakim."

He stopped.

"You could have called. It would have saved you an hour of driving here and back to Seattle."

"Then I would have foregone the pleasure of seeing you."

She looked ready to melt at that assurance and he smiled before walking away. His duty would be fulfilled very soon.

CHAPTER THREE

HAKIM took Catherine to his favorite restaurant on the waterfront for dinner. The ambiance was quiet and elegant. Perfect for proposing to his future wife.

He'd thought about taking her to the restaurant at the top of the Space Needle. He'd been told it was considered the height of romance, but sharing a noisy elevator with tourists on the way up held no appeal. At least not for tonight.

She smiled at him as he held her chair for her at the table. She'd worn a black dress with long sleeves, a peasant neckline and gathered waist. The full skirt swirled around her legs as she sat down. He let his fingers trail along the exposed skin of her shoulders above the wide neckline and she shivered. Satisfaction that his mission would soon be accomplished settled over him as he dropped his hand, moved around the table and took his own seat.

Even in the dim light of the restaurant, he could tell she was blushing again.

"Surely such a small touch is not cause for embarrassment?"

She smoothed her already perfectly coiffed hair. She'd worn it up again. Though he liked the view it gave him of her slender neck, one day soon, he would remove the clip and see what the dark honey strands looked like tumbling against her shoulders.

"I'm not embarrassed. Not exactly." Her sigh lifted

her breasts against the soft fabric of her bodice, revealing the source of her blush.

His little virgin was excited. Two unmistakable ridges under the black material gave her away. They also apprised Hakim of the fact she was not wearing a bra. The knowledge had a by now predictable effect on him.

"What are you exactly?" he asked, wondering if she would admit anywhere close to the truth.

"Stupid."

He shook his head. Little did she know, but her desire for him would soon be fulfilled. "Jewel of my heart, you must not say such things."

She dropped her focus to her lap, where she straightened her burgundy napkin against the black fabric of her skirt. "You shouldn't call me things like that. I know you're just saying it because it's the way you talk, but…"

He reached across the table to tip her chin up with his finger. "It is not merely the way I speak. Do I use such terms with other women in your hearing?"

Her bottom lip disappeared between her teeth and her eyes reflected confusion. "No." It was a bare whisper.

He wanted to kiss those trembling lips. Her vulnerability called to primitive instincts inside him.

"They are words meant for you alone."

It was as if she stopped breathing and she went utterly still, the look in her eyes a revelation of emotions so volatile he was shocked by them. Then her eyelashes lowered and she sucked in air too quickly, choking.

He offered her a glass of water as she sought to get the small coughing fit under control.

"Thank you." She drank the water and he watched as her throat convulsed gracefully with each swallow.

"You have a beautiful neck."

The water glass tumbled and only the quick action of a nearby waiter saved her dress from a drenching. Considering her reaction to his last statement, Hakim decided it would be best to wait until after dinner to propose.

By the time Hakim pulled his black car to a halt in the parking garage of her apartment building, Catherine's nerves were stretched tighter than an overtuned violin string. They wound one notch tighter when he insisted on seeing her inside.

She watched his dark hands as they unlocked her door and turned the knob to open it. Such masculine hands and yet so fluid in their movement, she desperately wanted them on her.

He pushed the door open and ushered her inside, one of the hands she found so fascinating secured around her waist. Her lungs stopped working while her heart went into overdrive. He closed the door and locked it, indicating he wasn't leaving any time soon and her already racing heart went turbocharged.

He led her toward the living room and she was surprised when her legs were able to move. She felt like her bones had all melted to jelly.

When they reached her bright yellow couch, he gently pushed her down onto the overstuffed cushions and then sat beside her. So close beside her that her shoulder was pressed against the hard wall of his chest. "I wish to speak with you."

"Oh," she squeaked.

He laid the hand that was not attached to her waist on her thigh, succeeding in surrounding her completely with his body and putting her on the verge of hyper-ventilating.

What would he do if she turned to him and did what she'd been longing to do for so long, touch the black silkiness of his hair and kiss the sensual line of his mouth? She clasped her hands firmly together in her lap to stop them from taking liberties that might end in her humiliated rejection.

For several seconds, neither of them spoke, the rush of air going in and out of her lungs at such a rapid rate the only sound in the room. He started to draw small circles on her thigh with his forefinger, sending aware-ness arcing up her leg and to the center of her being. She stifled a gasp of pleasure. She couldn't move. Nor could she look at him. Her attention was firmly fixed on that darkly tanned hand as it moved lazily against the black knit of her skirt.

Still he said nothing.

The quiet became unbearable. "Hakim?"

His silence beat against her and she sensed he wanted something from her, but she did not know what. Finally, when she could not tolerate one more second of the tortuous anticipation, she raised her head and tilted it backward to look at his face.

It was what he'd been waiting for. Eye contact.

Dark ebony bored into her. "You have enjoyed these past weeks in my company, have you not?"

"Yes."

"Am I a fool to believe you would like our associ-ation to continue?"

"No." She had to clear her throat before she could get more words out. Necessary words. "You could never be a fool."

"Then I would also not be out of bounds to hope you might want to deepen our relationship?"

He wanted to be her boyfriend? Her mind couldn't quite grasp the concept, but she nodded her head in agreement anyway.

"Yes, I would be out of bounds, or yes you want to deepen our relationship?"

"I want…" She forced her halted lungs to pull in a breath of air. "I want to deepen our relationship."

Would he kiss her now? The mere thought sent her pulse on a ride like a runaway stagecoach.

"Marry me."

She was daydreaming. She had to be.

But there was something wrong with the fantasy. "But you've never even kissed me."

"I have not had the right."

"What do you mean? Were you… Were you attached to someone else?"

"No, not that, but I was not as you put it *attached to you*, either. It would not have been right for me to kiss you before formal declarations were made."

Did he mean declarations of love? No. He'd said formal declarations. "Do you mean you have to be engaged in your country to kiss?"

His hand moved from her thigh to her cheek and he cupped it, his expression almost tender. "To kiss a virgin, yes."

Was her lack of experience so obvious? She supposed it was. "But this is not Jawhar."

"Nevertheless, I will treat you with the respect due you."

That was nice. "If I say I'll marry you, will you kiss me then?" This was by far the strangest daydream she had ever indulged in, only she knew on some level it was all too real.

A distinctly predatory light entered his obsidian eyes. "Yes."

"Yes," she repeated, not ready for the fantasy to end.

"You will marry me?"

"Yes." He couldn't really mean it and she would say just about anything to experience his mouth on hers. "Now you can kiss me."

He lowered his head, until his lips were centimeters from hers. "I can?"

"Yes." When he didn't close the gap, she said, "Please."

The kiss was as soft and fleeting as a butterfly flitting from one flower to another, but he did not move his head away and their breath continued to mingle.

The scent of his cologne mixed with a fragrance that could only be him. Male. It called to the primordial woman in her. She wanted to claim this man.

"Are you teasing me?" she asked, wondering why he had not kissed her again, more thoroughly.

"I am teasing myself."

His admission was flint to the gunpowder of her self-control. To say such a thing implied he wanted her and that was as exciting as having his body so close she could feel his heartbeat. She closed the gap of those few centimeters, her mouth locking to his with enthusiasm, if not skill.

He didn't seem to mind. His grip on her tightened and he took control of the kiss almost immediately. His mouth moved against hers, his tongue running along the seam of her lips. She opened her mouth on a small rush of air and he took possession of the interior. She'd thought of kissing like this before of course, but it had seemed messy.

It felt wonderful.

He tasted like the tiramisu he'd had for dessert at the restaurant. He also tasted like Hakim and it was a flavor she could not get enough of.

She moaned and sucked on his tongue.

He growled, his grip on her going painfully tight now and she found herself in his lap, her breasts pressed against his chest.

She wanted to touch him. She had to touch him. Her hands landed against his shoulders and stayed there for a full five seconds while the kiss went on and on. But just feeling the heat of him under her fingers was not enough. She wanted to explore.

First she let her fingers trail through his hair. It felt soft, almost like silk and she explored the shape of his head through it. He was so male, even his head felt a particularly masculine way to her searching fingers.

A sense of desperation, laced with fear that this would end soon and she would miss having touched the rest of his body, she brought her hands down on either side of his face, slowly sliding them toward his neck, then shoulders. With each centimeter of movement, she memorized the feel of his warm skin against the pads of her fingertips.

Sliding her hands down the polished cotton of his shirt, under his jacket, she outlined each muscle, each ridge and valley on the masculine torso so close to her own.

He shuddered and she rejoiced that she could affect him.

His hands were kneading her backside and she could feel a growing ridge of hardness under her hip.

In the back of her mind, she registered that meant he was getting excited which sent her emotions careening out of control and the impossible feelings she harbored for this magnificent man poured out through her lips and fingertips.

As if the release of her emotions had freed something in him, his ardor increased and the kiss went nuclear.

His tongue dueled with hers, demanding a submission she was only too willing to give. While he conquered her mouth, she tore at the buttons on his shirt, getting enough undone to slip her hand inside and feel the smooth, hot flesh of his naked chest. It was at that point that she accepted this was not a waking dream. No fantasy could possibly be this good.

And somehow because it was real, it was more. More intense. More feeling. More excitement. Almost too much.

She broke her mouth from his and sucked in air, trying to breath as her world spun around her in a kaleidoscope of feelings she had never experienced, but nonetheless recognized.

She wanted him.

Desperately.

"Do engaged people get to make love?" Her own boldness shocked her, but she waited tensely for his answer.

The kneading action on her bottom stopped and his forehead fell against hers. "No."

"Is it because I'm a virgin?" she asked, feeling tears of frustration already burning at the back of her eyes.

Hakim was going to wake up to whatever insanity had prompted his proposal and withdraw. And she would *still* be a virgin. Life was so unfair.

"It is true. This is part of it."

"But I don't want to be a virgin," she wailed and then felt mortified color drench her face, neck and even the breasts achingly aware of the proximity of his body.

He didn't laugh. He didn't even smile. He kissed her, hard and quick against her mouth. "We must wait."

"I can't."

He groaned like a drowning man going under for the last time. The hardness under her thigh twitched and his mouth locked with hers again, this time not waiting for her to open her lips, but forcing them apart for the entrance of his tongue.

His hand came up and cupped her breast, his thumb brushing over her achingly erect nipple. She arched into his touch while squirming her backside against his hard maleness. She loved him so much. Loved what he was doing to her. Loved the anticipation of more. For the first time in her life Catherine was glad she had never been with another man.

She wanted Hakim to be her first.

He kissed his way down her neck, stopping to suckle her rapid pulse beat. Arrows of pleasure shot through her limbs and she cried out at the wonder of it all.

Then his mouth was on her collarbone, his tongue caressing her in a way she had not expected. She went completely still when he pulled the stretch neckline of her dress down to expose her braless breasts.

He stopped moving, too, pulling back until he had an unfettered view of her exposed flesh. There was a lot on display. Her figure in no way resembled the boyish shapes so popular in today's media.

She felt another blush crawl up her skin as her senses prickled with heat and heady excitement.

Dark fingers caressed her pinkened flesh, making her moan and shake in response.

"So beautiful. So perfect." His words registered with the same sensual impact as his touch had done.

"I'm—" She'd meant to say something about how she was not exactly cover model slender, but he forestalled her with a finger against her lips.

"Exquisite. You are exquisite."

Then his head lowered, his lips touched her sensitized flesh and she lost her sense of place and time. He tasted her. All of her, covering each square centimeter of her naked curves with tantalizing attention. By the time he took one of her nipples into his mouth, she was shaking and inexplicable tears were running hotly down her temples and into her hair.

It was too much. The pleasure was too great.

"Hakim, darling, please!"

She didn't know what she was begging for, but he seemed to as his hand trailed down her body until it reached the hem of her skirt. His fingers brushed against her stocking clad leg and moved upward, slowly, ever so slowly.

Combined with his tasting of her breast, this tormenting slowness was driving her mad. But then his hot fingers were on the skin above the top of her stocking, curving toward her feminine center. His fingertip brushed against the silk of her panties where it covered her most tender flesh and sensation exploded inside her like a nuclear reactor.

Her body bowed. She screamed. She thought Hakim cursed, but she couldn't be sure. Nothing but the agonizing pleasure of her body was registering completely.

His hand slipped inside the waistband of her panties, down to flesh that had never, ever felt a man's touch and she cried out in an overload of sensation as he touched that bit of feminine flesh that other women talked about, but she had never even experimented with finding.

She went rigid and then shook in convulsions that were so strong, her muscles ached from supporting them.

He continued his ministrations until her entire body went limp from the strain.

He pulled her close to his chest, wrapping her in his embrace with strong, sure arms. The tears that had been a trickle became a torrent and she sobbed against his chest with as much abandon as she had given to her pleasure.

He comforted her, whispering soothing sounding words in a language she did not recognize. It didn't matter that she couldn't understand the words, their tone was what she needed.

"That was too much," she said between hiccuping sobs.

"It was more beautiful than the desert at sunrise," was his response.

"I love you," she confessed, her heart left unprotected by the amazing experience she had just gone through.

She was hopelessly in love with a man who could have any woman he wanted and that scared her. Refusing to admit it did not change it and there was a certain amount of relief in letting the truth out.

His hands caressed her back and she shivered with another convulsion. If it had been an earthquake, she would have called it an aftershock. It had been close enough.

He picked her up, carrying her as if she weighed no more than one of the throw pillows off the sofa. When they came into her bedroom, he flipped on the small light by her bed, casting a warm glow in the room.

Stopping beside the bed, he bent to lay her down, but she clung to his neck. "Please, don't leave."

She couldn't bear being alone after *that*.

He tensed.

"Please," she begged again.

"Do not plead. If you want me to stay, I will stay."

She let go of his neck and let him lay her down on the bed. He straightened to stand beside her. "Prepare yourself for bed and I will return to hold you."

"Aren't we going to make love?" she asked, not at all sure she could stand another dose of pleasure like what she had just gone through, but willing to try.

"Not until we are married."

She still didn't believe for a minute they were actually going to end up married. "But…" She could see the hard ridge still pressing against his slacks.

He shook his head decisively. "We will wait."

She couldn't expect him to hold her all night in that condition.

"I could…" She blushed without completing the offer, knowing he was a smart enough guy to figure it out.

"I'll take a shower."

"You're going to take a cold shower?" The thought of a sexy man like Hakim having to take a cold shower over her was somehow very appealing.

He smiled as if he could read her thoughts. "As you say. Prepare yourself for bed. I will return in but a moment."

She nodded and silently watched him walk into the en suite. It was only when she looked down that she realized her chest was still exposed. Her nipples were still hard and wet from his mouth. Oh my. The sight paralyzed her for a full minute before she was able to get up and find a nightgown to wear to bed.

Hakim stood under the warm jets of water, his body buffeted by the pain of unrequited passion, his mind filled with pleasure at how successfully his campaign had gone.

Catherine had agreed to be his wife.

His uncle would be pleased. Her father would be pleased. Hakim was pleased.

Marriage to Catherine would be no hardship.

Under the shy exterior, she was so passionate, so beautifully sensual. It had been harder than he ever would have thought possible to pull back from making love to her completely.

She'd liked that. His sweet little wallflower had liked thinking he was in here taking a cold shower because of his desire for her. The shower wasn't cold, but only because he'd never found that an effective deterrent to desire. He had found that warm water could sometimes soothe the physical ache of wanting what he could not yet have.

It wasn't working right now though. His sex was so hard, he was in pain.

He could not banish the image from his head of how she had looked with her dress pulled down, her breasts swollen and quivering with her desire. And the way she had exploded…her entire body bowing with such strong contractions, he had found it most difficult to keep his jewel on the couch. He groaned as his male member throbbed at the memories.

Maybe a cold shower would help.

Turning the knob all the way to the right, he was

soon blasted with an icy spray. He gritted his teeth, practicing a self-discipline technique he had learned while training with elite guard in his uncle's palace.

Catherine would have to marry him very soon.

She would not demur at a simple civil ceremony, he was certain. She was too happy to be marrying him.

She loved him.

Though it was not necessary, it pleased him, it pleased his pride that his future wife loved him.

Her shock at his proposal underscored the reality that she had reached the age of twenty-four without once having had a serious relationship, or even a steady date. Or so her father had asserted and Hakim had no reason to disbelieve him.

Her virginity had been an important issue to Hakim's uncle. According to the old man, no royal prince of Jawhar could marry a woman of uncertain morals. Hakim felt a certain primitive satisfaction in Catherine's untouched state, but he hardly placed the importance on it that his uncle did.

After all, he'd been prepared to marry once before and the woman had not been a virgin. Undoubtedly his uncle would not have approved.

And right now, when he wanted very much to bury himself in the silken wetness of Catherine's body, her innocence was more barrier to pleasure than benefit.

Reentering the bedroom, he found Catherine sitting up in the bed wearing a virginal, almost Victorian gown in white and her dark honey hair hanging over one shoulder in a thick braid. He smiled at her innocence.

As he got closer to the bed however, his smile slipped. He doubted very much that she realized it, but the gown was borderline sheer and the dark aureoles of her nipples were visible as well as the outline of her gorgeous breasts. He wished he'd left his slacks on as the benefits of the cold shower disappeared and the silk of his boxers shifted with his growing erection.

Catherine didn't seem to notice. Her blue eyes were unfocused as she stared at something beyond his right shoulder. Her lips were slightly parted and he could see the sweet, pink, enticing interior of her mouth.

As he climbed into the bed beside her, she jumped as if startled.

"Hakim!"

"You were not expecting me?"

Soft color flooded her cheeks and she scooted down into the bed so that the quilted spread covered her to her neck. "I was thinking about something."

"And was I this something?"

Expecting a shy affirmative, he was surprised and chagrined to see her shake her head in a jerky motion.

"What were you thinking of?"

She started. "Just, just a story that's all."

"A story?"

"Sometimes I like to tell stories in my head."

"Our lovemaking was not enough to keep your mind occupied?" The fact his innocent fiancée had been able to dismiss their lovemaking from her thoughts when he had not, irritated him.

"I didn't want to think about it."

Offended, he demanded, "Why not?"

And only realized as she pulled back that he was leaning over her in a most intimidating fashion. He did not move back however. He wanted an explanation.

"You said we couldn't make love until we're married."

"Yes. This is true."

"Well, then what would be the point of letting myself get all worked up if you aren't going to let anything happen?"

It was a good question. One he wished he could answer, but he had not been so successful in tamping down his own desires. He was rock hard and the only thing saving his pride were the blankets covering them both. Even so, had he not had his body tilted toward her, his erection would have tented the covers and given him away.

It shamed and frustrated him that his usual ice-cool restraint was letting him down. With all his training, she had more control over her desires than he did his. He did not like weakness, even that of a purely sexual nature.

"So you told a story in your head?" What sort of story would have been sufficient to take her mind off of the pleasure of their lovemaking?

"Yes."

"And it was not about me." He felt his irritation turn to irrational anger at the thought.

"That would defeat the purpose, wouldn't it?" Her tone said her words should be obvious to even the simplest of minds.

He glared at her. "I thought you wanted me to stay with you tonight."

Suddenly the pragmatic tilt to her mouth disappeared and searing vulnerability beamed at him from the startling blue of her eyes. "Yes. Are you going to leave because I was daydreaming?"

She had much to learn about him. "I made a commitment to stay. I will stay."

She chewed on her bottom lip, still red and full from his kisses. "Do you always keep your promises?"

"Always." He repeated the word in his mind, reminding himself he had given her his word to wait until their marriage to receive the gift of her purity.

CHAPTER FOUR

"IN OUR marriage, you will always know that when I promise a thing, it will be done."

Catherine stared at him. Their marriage? This joke had gone far enough. "Stop teasing. We're not really going to be married."

Hakim's black eyes snapped at her and the darkly dangerous side to his nature she had first suspected became all too real. "When you promise me something I expect the same from you. We will be married."

"But why?" It had to be obvious to him that he didn't have to marry her in order to make love to her. She was way too vulnerable to her desire for him and after what had happened on the couch, he had to know it.

He tapped the end of her nose with his forefinger. "Are you so uncertain of your own appeal you must ask this question?"

"But you're a sheikh for goodness' sake. Don't you have to marry a princess or something?"

"We are not quite so medieval in the royal family of Jawhar. Catherine, it is my desire to marry you."

A twenty-four-year-old children's librarian who had never even been kissed by a man before that night? "I don't think so."

The gentle touch of his palm against her cheek mesmerized her. "I want you, Catherine. I thought that was obvious."

Was it true? Felicity had told Catherine many times

45

that she was no longer the girl too tall for her age or whose face was pockmarked with severe acne. But Catherine had never stopped feeling like that girl.

He tilted her head toward him. "Accept that it pleases me very much to make you my wife."

But why did it please him? The only logical answer that she could think of was so beyond the realm of reality, she felt shock thrill through her even contemplating it. Yet, she could think of only one reason for a man like Hakim to marry a woman like her. She had no diplomatic pull, could not increase his cache with his people and while her father was wealthy, Hakim was wealthier.

Love.

He had to love her. It was the only thing that made any sense of their situation. He'd never said the words, but maybe that was a cultural thing. Or an alpha guy, totally in charge and too cool to admit to really tender emotions kind of thing. Whatever.

When she remained silent, stunned by the thoughts racing through her mind, he sighed and rolled onto his back. "The time has come for me to marry. It is my uncle's wish I marry now."

"And you picked me."

"You are my chosen bride, yes."

She thought of the years since her laser treatments during which her father had thrown men at her head, men interested only in what they would gain materially from the marriage. Men who had not stirred her emotions or her senses as Hakim did. Not only did he stir her emotions, he returned them.

A glorious smile broke over her face. "I want children." Family who would love her and accept her love unconditionally.

"As do I."

Then a sudden thought assailed her, one she could not dismiss. Not when he'd withheld the words of love so there was this little niggle of doubt way down, deep inside. "You have to be faithful. No mistresses. No other wives."

He didn't smile, didn't make a joke of it as some men would have. In fact, his expression turned even more serious, his mouth set grimly. "Polygamy is not practiced in Jawhar and to take a mistress would be to compromise my own honor as a prince among my people."

"Then I will marry you." Even as she said the words, she had a hard time believing them.

"Then I am content."

The words were a little disappointing. *I am content* did not sound nearly as romantic as *I love you*, but what did she expect with a sophisticated guy like Hakim? A brass band?

"It is time we slept." He kissed her briefly and it was all she could do not to follow his lips as they pulled away from hers.

"All right."

Although, he did not pull her into his body, he did lay one arm across her stomach and it felt so nice, she wasn't even tempted to slip into fantasizing herself to sleep. For once, reality outshone anything her imagination could conjure.

A featherlight touch on his cheek woke Hakim. He waited to open his eyes to see what she would do.

Her small hand settled on his chest, her fingertips touching his collarbone. And then nothing. No movement of any kind, but he could feel her gaze as if it were an electric current directed at him. Opening his eyes, he found her looking not at his face, but at her hand against his chest.

"Good morning."

Her gaze rose to his and the wonder in the blue depths of her eyes did strange things to him. "Good morning, Hakim."

She was closer than she had been last night, her warm, womanly body pressed against his length and his morning erection tightened to urgent need in the space of a heartbeat. She could not help but notice, the small gasp and perfect "O" of her lips confirming she had indeed felt his body's response to her nearness.

He needed to move away. Immediately.

This was much too dangerous.

"Do you…"

He waited for her to finish her question, but she didn't. Instead, her hand, which had been immobile for several minutes, now started a slow slide down his chest.

He should stop her. He knew he should stop her, but that hesitant little hand turned him on as no woman performing the *raqs sharqi* after years training in belly dancing had ever done. He waited with heart-stopping impatience for her hand to reach its destination. She stopped when her fingertips reached the top of his boxer shorts. He would not ask her to continue, but waiting to see if she did so was driving him wild.

One tentative fingertip outlined the hard ridge. His sex twitched. Her exclamation drowned out his moan. She yanked her hand back and rolled away from him. Her breath was coming out in little pants.

She stared up at the ceiling, her fingers gripping the blankets with white-knuckle intensity. "I've read romance novels, you know? Some of them have pretty steamy love scenes.''

''And?''

''Experiencing it is different than reading about it.'' She sounded so perplexed, he smiled.

''Yes.''

''I mean, I didn't expect to be so nervous.''

''You are a virgin, little kitten.''

Her head turned and gentian blue eyes pinned him. ''Why do you call me that?''

''Your name.''

''My name?''

''Catherine. Cat. Only you do not act like a cat. You are more like a kitten. Inquisitive. Sometimes shy. Innocent.''

''Oh. Are all virgins so jumpy about touching male flesh?''

He did not know. He had never bedded one. ''You did not touch my flesh.''

Catherine whipped over to face him fully.

Her braid landed heavily against her unfettered breast and he found his attention riveted by the hardened nipples pressing against the almost transparent fabric of her nightgown. So he did not catch her words at first. His brain had to play them back for him to make sense of them.

She had said, ''I did touch you.''

He reached out and brushed the back of his fingers against the nipple that tantalized him so. ''This is touching you through your gown.'' Then he untied the ribbon holding the neckline of her gown together, slowly pulling the ends until the bow unraveled.

She stopped breathing.

He parted the edges of the gown and gently cupped her naked breast, palming the excited peak.

"Oh, my gosh!"

He could not quite smile. He was in too much pain from his need, but he felt the smile inside. She was so responsive to him. So perfect. "This is touching your flesh."

Her, "Oh," came out choked.

He knew he was teasing them both because he did not believe he could give her completion without taking her. His control was too close to the edge. Yet, he tormented himself playing with her nipples and caressing the swollen skin around them.

"Can I... Can I..." She repeated the phrase with each rotation of his hand, but did not complete her thought.

"Can you what?"

"Touch your flesh." The word *flesh* came out a long, soft moan.

He wanted it. He wanted it very much, but if she did, they would consummate their marriage before the wedding. This would be wrong. He had made a promise. He must keep it. His mind knew the truth, but his libido argued that this was America, not Jawhar. She did not care about the standards to be adhered to by a sheikh of his people, would not care if he broke his word on this.

"It would not be wise."

"*Hakim.*" Her tortured cry was loud in the silent room.

He reluctantly pulled his hand from her soft curve, moving to lie on his back. He felt as if he had been hiking in the desert under the noonday sun.

"You go to my head." He should not admit such a

thing. It gave her power over him. Her innocence and eager response to him was too much of a temptation.

Her soft laugh had him turning his head to look at her. Her smile was that of an imp. "I was under the impression I *went to* other parts of your body."

"That too."

She looked so happy with herself, he was tempted to kiss the lips curved so sweetly. Then a wrinkle formed between her eyebrows and she frowned as if in thought. "Are you sure it's me?"

"I see no one else in the room."

She bit her bottom lip. "I mean, I read that men wake up feeling that way. Maybe it was just your normal morning reaction, you know?"

He couldn't help it. He burst out laughing.

The uncertainty in her gaze contained his mirth. He reached out to brush her cheek because he could not prevent himself. "You know book knowledge, but as you said earlier, the reality is quite different. I want you, Catherine, I am throbbing with need, I assure you."

That had her smiling again. "Good."

Hakim had been gratifyingly complimentary over the Belgian waffles and scrambled eggs seasoned with her own special combination of spices that Catherine had made for breakfast. It was the first time she'd made breakfast for a man. The entire morning had been filled with firsts for her. The first time waking up beside a man. The first time she had to share a toothbrush. She'd been surprised when the fastidious Hakim had so calmly asked to use hers.

It had seemed like such an intimate thing to do.

Like what they'd done on the sofa and then in her bed hadn't been, she chided herself.

She finished putting the dishes in the apartment's small dishwasher while Hakim wiped down the counters and table.

"You're awfully domesticated for a sheikh."

"I lived alone for most of my university years."

"You said most, does that mean you had a roommate for a while?" Her mind boggled at the thought of rooming with a sheikh. Of course she would be doing that soon. As his wife.

His expression closed. "Yes. I had a roommate for a while." He tossed the dishcloth in the sink.

She rinsed it, wrung it out and hung it over the sink divider. "It didn't work out, huh?"

She could remember horror stories from friends at college who had shared their dorm rooms with impossible people.

"No. It did not work out."

Something in his voice alerted her that he wasn't talking about getting rid of a roommate because he was a slob.

"Was it a woman?" she asked before thinking better of it.

Hakim's face tightened. "Yes."

She had to know more. "Were you a couple?"

"Yes," he said again, but offered nothing more.

She swallowed an inexplicable lump in her throat. "Was it serious?"

"We considered marriage."

"But you broke up."

"She did not fancy life in a backwater like Jawhar." The way he said the words, Catherine got the impression he was quoting the faceless woman he had once considered marrying verbatim.

"But you live in Seattle."

"At the time, my plans were to return to my homeland."

"She refused to go with you?" Catherine was incredulous. How could any woman who loved him turn down a lifetime with Hakim, no matter where they lived?

"Yes. When do you plan to tell your parents of our engagement?"

Knowing he had loved another woman enough to want marriage hurt, even though she knew it shouldn't and she was more than willing to go along with his abrupt change in conversation.

Nevertheless, his question caught her unawares. Tell her parents? What would happen if he backed out? She still couldn't quite believe Hakim wanted her, wanted to marry her.

Stop it right there, she firmly told herself.

She wasn't going to live in fear of rejection for the rest of her life. She had to stop reacting like the emotionally scarred preadolescent or physically scarred teenager she had been and start acting like the future wife of a sheikh.

"I can tell my mother this morning."

A strange expression crossed his face. "What of your father?"

That would concern Hakim. Parental approval was a big thing in his culture…in hers too, really. They just went about different ways of getting it. He asked beforehand while she'd learned it was easier to get her parents blessing on a project than their permission before starting it.

She looked at the clock which read seven-thirty. "He's already at work, but Mom will be home for another couple of hours."

"Then let us call her."

They did and Lydia Benning was ecstatic at the news her youngest daughter was finally getting married. Catherine grimaced at the phone. *Twenty-four was not that old.*

"You'll have to bring him for dinner tonight. I'll call right now and invite Felicity and Vance," she said, naming Catherine's sister and brother-in-law. "I can't wait to welcome the man who wants to marry my little girl. He's a sheikh—that's just so romantic."

After gushing for another full five minutes, she cut the connection.

Catherine smiled at Hakim. "I hope you don't mind, but I've agreed to dinner at my parents' house tonight."

"So I gathered. I will pick you up here."

"We could just meet there. They don't live all that far from your penthouse building."

"I'll be here at six-thirty to escort you."

"So, she's agreed has she?" Harold Benning made no effort to disguise the satisfaction he felt at the news Hakim had recently imparted. His brown eyes fairly sparked with it.

"Yes."

Harold's hands rubbed together. Of average height, he had the look of one of his miners. Even his suit, made by an exclusive London tailor, did little to hide the raw musculature of Hakim's soon-to-be father-in-law. He looked like what he was, an extremely wealthy self-made man.

He never apologized for that fact, either. At no time during negotiations with the King of Jawhar had Harold Benning showed the least discomfiture at the prospect of his daughter married to the Sheikh of Kadar.

Hakim wondered briefly how such a self-assured man could have raised Catherine, who was so insecure.

"You haven't told her about our little arrangement, have you?"

"No."

"Good." Harold's graying red head bobbed twice in acknowledgment. "She wouldn't understand. Her mother and I have been concerned about her lack of a social life for quite a while. Sure, it was understandable when she was younger, but since the laser treatments, she's been as reclusive as ever. And she balks at every attempt Lydia and I make to introduce her to men."

Laser treatment? He would have to ask Catherine about that. "She sets great store by her independence." Something that would naturally change with their marriage.

"Yes, that she does. She can be stubborn."

Hakim could not picture the shy Catherine being willful, but did not bother to disagree with her father. "Is your wife aware of the arrangement between my uncle and your company?"

Tugging at his collar, Harold grimaced. "Not exactly. I told her I was looking to fix a husband up for Catherine, but she wouldn't understand the business side of it any better than my daughter. Women are romantics at heart, the lot of them."

"You would know your family best." His sister knew to the coin how much dowry money had exchanged hands upon her marriage to a prince in their mother's father's Bedouin tribe.

Yet, she had been brilliantly happy on her wedding day. He wanted his bride to be equally pleased and if keeping certain details from her was conducive to such happiness, that was what he would do.

CHAPTER FIVE

HAKIM approved of the understated décor and Queen Anne furnishings in the Benning's Seattle mansion. Catherine's mother, Lydia, had excellent taste and it showed from the gloss black grand piano in the living room to the subdued upholstery on the dining room chairs.

They were in the dining room now, just finishing dessert. The evening had been illuminating. Catherine's mother and sister could have been twins with their petite builds, pale blond hair and gray eyes. And while Catherine and her sister were obviously close, there was a distance between mother and daughter he found disturbing.

Despite this, Lydia Benning appeared genuinely pleased her daughter was happy. *And Catherine was happy.* It radiated off her in waves, her enticing lips constantly curving in one sexy smile after another.

He watched as she took a bite of her crème brûlée, his temperature spiking when she closed her eyes and licked the spoon.

There was a small bit of burnt sugar on the corner of her lips and he reached out to gently wipe it away with his fingertip. She went still at his touch and suddenly what had been simple became complicated as her eyes reflected the desire he felt.

Laughter around them broke the sensual link.

''The wedding had better take place soon, if that

look means anything.'' Vance's voice was full of amusement.

Hakim agreed with the sentiment completely. "I believe the waiting period in the state of Washington is one week."

"Actually it's three days." Catherine's voice was husky. "But what difference does that make? It will take at least six weeks to put together a church wedding."

Hakim turned to face his fiancée. Their eyes met again, hers had gone the color of the night sky in the desert. "Do you really want a formal wedding?"

She was much too shy to desire to be the center of attention at such a gathering.

"Why not?"

Her question shocked him. "Have you forgotten the meeting of the Antique Telescope Society we attended together?"

She looked puzzled. "What does that have to do with our wedding?"

"You refused to examine the telescope because it required going up in front of the others to do so." She had denied that was the case, but it had been obvious her shyness had held her back. "You shook like you'd been standing in the cold when you gave that small speech at the charity reception. You would be a nervous wreck put on display in front of several hundred wedding guests."

The glow of happiness surrounding her dimmed a little. "You want to marry in a civil ceremony?"

Perhaps the thought of being wed by a judge did not sit well with her. "We can arrange a midweek ceremony with a clergyman if you prefer."

Her eyes flickered, but she did not smile in gratitude as he expected. In fact, her smile disappeared altogether.

"You don't mind being married in a church?" Vance asked.

Hakim looked away from Catherine reluctantly, disturbed by her sudden lack of animation.

"My grandfather's tribe is one of the many Bedouin tribes converted to Christianity centuries ago."

"But I thought all the Bedouins had converted to Islam," Felicity remarked.

"Not all." Hakim didn't really want to get into a discussion of religious history among the Bedouin people. He wanted Catherine to smile again. "You are all right with a small ceremony?" he asked her.

Catherine thought a certain amount of arrogance must be bred into men like Hakim. Even his question came out like a command.

What could she say? That she had dreamt of her wedding since she was a little girl? That those dreams had not included a poky wedding held in the middle of the day in the middle of the week with only family as guests?

He was right. Considering the way she reacted to being the center of attention, there was no reason for him to have suspected she wanted anything more than a few words spoken in a judge's chamber.

But her dreams were not limited by her fears and knowing that Hakim wanted to marry her had given her confidence. He was a special guy. Sexy. Gorgeous. He was a sheikh, for Heaven's sake. And he loved her. That knowledge had given her a desire to fulfill the secret dreams of her heart.

Before she could answer, he reached out and touched

her. His look was intimate and full of promise. "I want to make you my wife."

The unspoken message was clear. He wanted to make love to her and he'd already said that would have to wait until after the ceremony.

She wanted him, too, even more than the fairytale wedding trappings. She forced a smile. "All right."

"Catherine!" Felicity's voice registered shock and a certain amount of disappointment.

Felicity would have fought for the flowers. In fact, she had. Not that Vance had even hinted at anything less than a full production when they'd gotten married, but then he had loved her sister. He had not even balked at Felicity's insistence on having her sister for a bridesmaid. At the time, Catherine's face had looked like she had a perpetual case of severe chicken pox.

In the end, it had been Catherine who begged her sister to allow her to be the candle lighter instead. She hadn't wanted to stand in front of a church full of people during the ceremony or be in any of the wedding photos. Her mother had been more than willing to give instructions to that effect to the photographer.

Shaking off the painful memories, Catherine smiled reassuringly at her older sister. "You can help me put it together."

Felicity's mouth opened and shut, her porcelain fine features drawn in lines of rejection. "Sweetie, you wanted a horse drawn carriage, oodles of flowers, music—"

Catherine cut in before her sister exposed her childish fantasies completely. "That was when I was nine years old." A year before she'd become *Amazon Girl*, growing five inches in one summer and towering above her classmates the following September. Boys and girls alike. For one reason or another, the next ten years had been hell on Catherine's self-confidence.

"But—"

"Do you want to go shopping with me tomorrow? I need a wedding dress."

That caught her sister's attention. "Of course, but don't you have to work at the library?"

"I'll take a personal day." She'd never taken one. She was due the concession.

"What about a honeymoon?" Vance asked.

Catherine shook her head decisively. "Not possible."

"Why not?" Hakim asked. He had planned to take her to Jawhar immediately to meet his family.

"I can't leave the library in the lurch like that. We don't have enough time to schedule someone to cover all of my shifts."

"That's ridiculous. I'll hire a temp if that's what you need," Harold inserted, his first contribution to the wedding plans.

Catherine shook her head. "Reference Desk librarians don't generally hire out through temporary agencies, Dad."

"You could always quit your job." Lydia smiled tentatively at her daughter. "Hakim will need your attention once you are married. You'll want to establish a firmer social footing."

Hakim agreed with Lydia. Not necessarily about the social scene, but he wanted to come first in his wife's priorities. The narrowing of Catherine's eyes and straight line of her mouth said she did not think much of her mother's suggestion.

"I'm not quitting my job," she said tightly, "I like it."

"And if I told you that was what I wanted?" Hakim

asked, testing how much in common his fiancée had with his former live-in lover in regard to the importance they placed on their careers.

"Is that what you want?" she asked, turning the tables back on him and giving nothing away with her expression.

"I would like to know you are available to travel with me when the need arises."

"With sufficient notice, I can travel with you now."

And one week was not sufficient notice. "Then we will have to plan a trip to Jawhar after you've given proper notification for your vacation time at the library. I want you to meet my family."

"Won't they be coming for the wedding?" Felicity accepted a fresh glass of wine from her husband. "Surely your parents would not want to miss it."

"There is only my sister. She and her husband will be delighted to meet my new wife when we travel to the desert of Kadar."

"Don't you have any other family?" Felicity asked.

"Some. There is my mother's father. He is the sheikh of a Bedouin tribe." He paused. "There is also my father's brother, the King of Jawhar, as well, and his family."

"Your uncle is a king?" Felicity demanded, her eyes round.

"Yes." He caught Catherine's hand to his mouth and kissed the small circle of her palm. "Grandfather will be pleased. He has been encouraging me to marry since I graduated from university."

Of course the old man had thought marriage would bring Hakim home to the desert and it would not.

"Why can't your family come?" Felicity asked, clearly unwilling to drop the subject.

Grimness settled over him. "There is a faction of dissidents in Jawhar that oppose my uncle's leadership. He fears to leave the country now would be to put it at risk from this group of rebels."

"But I thought your family had been the ruling sheikhs for generations." Catherine's expression was clouded with confusion. "It seems odd there would be serious opposition after all these years. Your uncle is loved among the people of Jawhar."

She had been studying his country. The knowledge pleased him. "This is true. Nevertheless, dissension arises from time to time. Twenty years ago, there was an attempted coup. It failed, but many were left dead." Like his parents he thought bitterly.

"What does that have to do with today?" she asked.

"The remnant which survived that attempt have been gathering forces outside Jawhar for the past five years. My uncle is concerned they will once again attempt a removal of our family from power. He cannot risk leaving the country, nor can my cousins."

"What about your sister?"

"She is married to the man that will one day succeed my grandfather as sheikh of his tribe and will meet you when we travel to the desert for our Bedouin marriage ceremony."

Catherine's eyes widened. "We're going to be married a second time in Jawhar?"

"Yes." It would be necessary to fulfill his obligation of respect toward his grandfather.

Catherine was quiet in the car on the way to her apartment. She and Hakim were to go for the wedding license the first thing the next morning. She was still finding it difficult to assimilate that bit of information.

And her mind continued to play with images of long

ago dreams. Lights flickered over the dark interior of
the car as Hakim passed a semitruck on the freeway,
but it barely registered as Catherine's thoughts slipped
into a fantasy of the perfect wedding.

She was standing at the altar in a gown of the most
exquisite lace and Hakim looked at her the way a man
in love gazed at the woman he was about to marry. That
was definitely a dream. They were surrounded by can-
dles and flowers. Bunches and bunches of flowers, all
white, all in perfect bloom.

A soft sound escaped her lips.

"What are you thinking, Catherine?"

She was so lost in her daydream, she answered without thought. "Flowers. Lots and lots of flowers."

Then she realized what she'd said and felt the warmth
steal into her cheeks. At least he would not notice in
the dim interior of the car.

Hakim sighed. "Tell me about the horse drawn carriage and oodles of flowers your sister mentioned."

"It was just something we used to talk about when
we were little."

"And something you were thinking about just now."
He sounded resigned. "Tell me, Catherine. I want to
hear."

Why not? He'd asked. It wasn't as if she was demanding they go through with her long ago plans. "Felicity and I used to talk about what our dream weddings
would be like. I think a lot of little girls imagine themselves in a beautiful gown, riding in a carriage with
Prince Charming at their side. It was all just silly fantasy, nothing that applies to this marriage."

"Am I not your Prince Charming?"

She couldn't help smiling at the question as she was
sure she was meant to. "Well. You are a prince in

Jawhar and you are charming, so I suppose it would be appropriate to call you my Prince Charming.''

"So, it is only the fantasy wedding you find impossible.''

"It's not something you can throw together in a week." She couldn't help the slight wistfulness in her tone.

"It is something that takes a minimum of six weeks?''

He had remembered her comment from dinner.

"I don't know." She'd never planned one and Felicity's wedding had been organized over several months.

"With sufficient financial and manpower resources at your disposal, do you think you could put together this dream wedding in less than six weeks?''

"How much less?" What was he getting at?

"Could you do it in under a month?''

"Are you saying you're willing to wait?''

"It pleases me to make your dreams come true." He sounded so arrogant, but could she blame him?

He *was* making her dreams come true.

"Three weeks?" she asked, as if she were bartering a deal.

"You will take sufficient time off after the wedding to visit Jawhar?''

With three weeks' notice, she could arrange it…just. "Yes.''

His smile flashed. "Then it is a deal.''

The engagement dinner was more like a party. Her mother had invited a hundred of her nearest and dearest, arranging for the meal to take place in an upscale Seattle restaurant with a live orchestra and dance floor.

Catherine circled the floor in her father's arms and listened while he listed off Hakim's attributes.

"Boy's got a good head for business on his shoulders."

She wondered how her sheikh would feel being referred to as a boy. Suppressing a smile, she nodded her agreement.

"He's considerate. Look at how he changed his mind about the wedding."

Finally her amusement found vent in a small laugh. "Dad, you don't have to sell Hakim to me. He's not one of your matchmaking attempts." *Thankfully.* "I chose him and he chose me. I want to marry him."

Satisfaction coursed through her at the knowledge that her father had had nothing to do with her and Hakim meeting. She wasn't a pity date, or being eyed as a possible way into her father's good graces. Hakim wanted nothing from her father, needed nothing from Benning Mining and Excavations. His desire for her might be physical, but at least it was for her. He wanted her, Catherine Marie Benning, and nothing else.

Hakim waited for his bride at the front of the church. Organ music swelled and he turned to face the massive oak doors at the back of the church. They swung wide and Catherine's sister came into view. Hakim felt shock lance through him. The filmy fabric of her dress was the color of a robin's egg, but that was not what held Hakim motionless. It was the *al-firdous* style of the dress. It had been embroidered and beaded in traditional Middle Eastern patterns with thread and beads the same color as the dress. Felicity wore the matching sheer scarf looped over her pale blond hair much the same way his own sister would have done.

Hakim felt his pulse increase as he waited to see his bride. He barely noticed the flower girl as she came forward, dropping rose petals along the white runner, or the small boy wearing a traditional tuxedo bearing the rings.

Each of the attendants had taken their place when the music halted for the count of several seconds. When it began again, the organ played the strains of the "Wedding March." And then she was there, framed by the open portal of the two massive doors. Hakim's mouth went dry. She had brought together east and west with mind-numbing effect.

The traditional white wedding gown fit snuggly against her body, accentuating the feminine curves to her hips and then flared out in a skirt that rustled as she made the slow march toward him. But the hem, the edges of the medieval sleeves and the off the shoulder neckline had all been embroidered with gold geometric patterns. The semitransparent veil had matching embroidery around its edges, a veil worn in the tradition of his homeland covering all but the exquisite gentian blue of her eyes. Which as she came closer he could see had been outlined with kohl, giving his shy little flower a look of mystery.

Her lips were curved in a smile behind the soft white chiffon covering her face. She reached his side and her father put her hand into Hakim's. He curled his fingers around hers. Her skin was cold and the hand holding her white bouquet was shaking. He squeezed, offering the assurance of his presence. She had wanted this large wedding, but that did not mean a lifetime of shyness had dissolved in a fortnight.

They spoke their vows, he in a firm steady voice, she almost in a whisper. Then he was sliding a white gold band to accompany the large ruby in a Bedouin setting he had given her after she agreed to marry him. The ring had belonged to his mother.

The pastor gave Hakim permission to kiss his bride and everything around them faded to nothing as he reached out to unhook her veil and expose her face. He did it slowly, wanting to savor the moment of unveiling. Then he lowered his head until their lips barely brushed.

He liked this particular Western wedding custom. Her mouth parted slightly and he pulled her to him for a kiss that staked his claim on the beautiful woman before him for all the wedding guests to see.

When Hakim lifted his head, he knew his sense of satisfaction and accomplishment radiated off of him.

He had fulfilled his duty and had for a wife a woman who would satisfy his passions.

He was content.

"What are you thinking about, Catherine?"

Catherine turned from the window whose only view was a night-darkened sky and smiled at Hakim. "Nothing."

She'd been thinking about the night ahead, but could not have said so to save her life.

He'd been in the cockpit with the pilot for takeoff which had given her some much needed moments to herself. Ever since he had informed her there was a bedroom on the plane, with the implication they would make use of it, she had been vacillating between fear and anticipation.

She wasn't sure which one she was feeling now. "Tell me, will you insist on overseeing the landing as well?" she asked to avoid the probing look in his dark as night eyes.

He shrugged broad shoulders. "Probably."

"Your uncle's pilots must love flying you."

He flashed her a smile. "They have made no complaints in the past, but then I had been content to remain in the cabin for takeoffs and landings."

"So, what's so special about this flight?"

"You need to ask? My wife is on the plane. I must always see to her safety."

Emotion caught in her throat and she had to take a deep breath before speaking. Sometimes she forgot he didn't love her and basked in the feelings his naturally protective nature caused. "Your wife is a lucky woman to be so well looked after."

His hand cupped her cheek and anticipation overwhelmed fear in the space of a heartbeat.

"I am hoping she thinks this is so."

"She does." Involuntarily her head turned and her lips kissed the center of his palm. The scent of his skin and the warmth of it against her lips tantalized her senses. "I do."

He leaned across her and unbuckled her seat belt. Taking her hand, he pulled gently until she stood. "Come little kitten, we have a bed that awaits our pleasure."

Was it just her, or did his speech become more eastern when his passion was engaged?

She nodded, her throat too tight to speak. It was time.

It occurred to her that she should have gone to the bedroom earlier, so she could greet him in the sensuous white satin nightgown Felicity had given her to wear tonight, but that was not to be. Catherine wasn't sure how she felt about that. Part of her was a bundle of nerves at the thought of parading herself in front of him in something so revealing. Another part of her did not wish to miss out on any of the traditional aspects to her wedding night.

Which was a silly response probably, so she said nothing.

He led her into the small bedroom at the back of the plane and she stopped, stock still, unable to believe her eyes. The bed was the first thing to arrest her interest. It was covered with quilted silks and tasseled pillows. There were flowers everywhere, all white and red. A silver ice bucket with a bottle of champagne stood beside the bed and red silk scarves covered the wall-mounted lights, giving a warm but subdued glow to the room.

"It is to your liking?"

Her eyes misted over. "Oh, yes. It's just beautiful." She turned to face him.

Heat radiated from his eyes. "I am glad to have pleased you. For today you have given me great delight."

"You liked the dress." She smiled. She'd known he would.

His hands settled on the shoulders of her bright blue suit jacket. "I loved the dress, but right now I would like very much to see you without even this most charming outfit you chose for traveling in."

She looked down at the suit and then back at Hakim. "You want me to take it off?" Somehow she had pictured him doing that for her.

"You have something else you would like to change into?" He sounded like he wouldn't mind seeing that nightgown Felicity bought her after all.

She looked around the small room uncertainly. Did he expect her to disrobe in front of him?

"There is a bathroom through there." He indicated

a door in the wall of the bedroom. "However, you would be more comfortable changing in here, I think. I will make use of it to undress."

He'd seen her practically naked, but her nerves didn't recognize that salient fact and she smiled her gratitude at him.

CHAPTER SIX

HAKIM came out of the tiny bathroom, having given his bride time to prepare for him.

Catherine sat in the middle of the bed surrounded by several Turkish pillows. Her glorious hair was unbound for the first time of their acquaintance and its dark honey strands cascaded over her shoulders.

She had her arms locked around her drawn up knees and the expression on her face was rueful. "I didn't know if I should be standing or lying down. So, I compromised and sat."

"Are you embarrassed for me to see your body?"

She shook her head causing her hair to ripple and he felt an instant reaction coursing through his body.

"Yet you are curled up like a small kitten."

"Small?" She laughed. "Perhaps you haven't noticed, but I'm a good deal taller than most women."

"Surely not. You are perhaps a shade above average in height, but to me, you are quite small." He wished he understood this tendency she had to refer to herself as if she were a giant.

"Yes, well, you are pretty tall aren't you?" The fact seemed to please her.

He shrugged. "Truthfully, among my people I am considered so." He had not thought to spend any portion of his wedding night discussing their relative heights, but if it relaxed her, he was willing to be tolerant.

"Kids used to tease me when I was little. They called me Amazon Girl, beanpole and other horrible names."

He sat down on the bed and laid one hand over her clasped ones. "Talk to me."

"I don't want to ruin tonight with bad memories."

He wanted to banish the remembered torment in her eyes. "Share these memories and I will help you dispel them."

"You're so confident."

So she had said before, or rather that he was arrogant. He shrugged. "I am a man."

She shook her head.

"I assure you this is true."

She laughed softly. "I'm not doubting you."

Unable to resist, he reached out and let a swath of her hair slip through his fingers. "Tell me." He waited in silence while she made up her mind to do so.

"When I was a little girl, I grew five inches in one summer. I didn't stop growing until I was taller than all the other children at school. I was thirteen then and some of the boys were beginning to catch up, but I remained taller than most of them for at least another year."

"It happens to many girls, it's not so bad."

"*It was.* I suppose it's hard for you to understand, but I went to co-ed school. The boys teased me about being a giant and the girls pitied me. I was shy and didn't make friends easily anyway, my sudden height just made everything worse."

"But as you say, the boys grew taller and the girls— many of them—would have caught up."

She shut her eyes. "I don't want to talk about this anymore."

There was something else. Something she did not

want to share, but he had a need to know everything about this woman he had married. A memory teased his conscious. "Your father said something about laser treatments. What were they for?"

She looked confused and not at all happy. "When did he mention them?"

Remembering the conversation, Hakim considered how best to answer without revealing his secret and could see no way of doing so and speak only the truth. There was a proverb among his people, *lying in its proper place is equal to worship*. It applied now. "We were discussing the upcoming wedding."

His lie was one of omission only.

"Oh." A look of profound sadness crossed her features. "When I was thirteen, I started to get acne."

"This is not unusual for an adolescent."

"No, but mine was horrible. The doctors tried antibiotics, acne skin treatments...the works. Nothing helped. My face was discolored with the purple scars from acne and fresh breakouts for five long years. The fresh breakouts finally cleared up when I was eighteen and I started the laser treatments on the scarring when I was nineteen."

He rubbed his thumbs along the perfect smoothness of her cheeks. "You are beautiful."

She grimaced. "Hardly that, but I'm no longer a social embarrassment to my parents and an object of pity to my peers."

Tension snaked through him at her words. "Surely your parents were not concerned about your looks to that extent."

She shrugged, but it was anything but a casual gesture. "They couldn't make it better, so they ignored the problem."

He sensed there was more to it than that and remained silent, hoping she would share it with him.

She looked into his eyes for several seconds, hers glazed with memories he could not see. But he could feel the pain of their impact in her.

Then she spoke. "There was only one way for them to close their eyes to the problem and that was to avoid me as much as possible. We didn't take family photos for those five years. They frequently entertained away from home rather than risk having their disfigured daughter the cynosure of all eyes."

Her eyes shone with tears she blinked away. "Felicity was the only one who didn't let it matter. She often invited me to stay with her and tried to help me out of the shell I'd crawled into to avoid possible rejection."

The picture Catherine painted was a chilling one.

"What happened after the laser treatments?"

"They went on a campaign to get me married. I think they believed that once I got a husband it would prove their genes weren't damaged after all."

"You resisted." Harold had said Catherine had refused to consider any of the men he'd brought to her attention.

"I didn't want pity dates or to be married as a means to an end in procuring a rich and influential father-in-law."

Hakim's body tensed. "I do not want your father's wealth."

Her smile was dazzling. "I know."

He could never tell her of the plans associated with their marriage. She would not understand. But he could show her what a desirable woman she was now, erasing the painful perceptions shaped by her past.

He stood up beside the bed and looked down at her. She tilted her head back and returned his gaze.

"You said you were not embarrassed for me to see you."

"I'm not."

He put his hand out to her. "Then come."

She hesitated only a fraction of a second before placing her small hand trustingly in his and allowing him to pull her up from the bed.

Sleek, shimmering white satin settled around the generous curves of her body, accentuating each dip and hollow in a way that sent his thoughts scattering to the four winds.

Forcing himself into movement, he turned and poured a glass of champagne. He took a sip of the bubbling wine and then grasped her shoulder, pulling her body into his so that the gentle roundness of her bottom pressed against his thighs. He placed the glass against her lips at the exact spot from which he had sipped.

"Share with me."

She allowed him to pour the champagne onto her tongue and then she swallowed. His hand drifted from her shoulder to cup her left breast. The nipple beaded against his palm, straining against the silky fabric and she let out a small moan.

He fed her another sip of champagne while squeezing the soft flesh in his hand. He continued the sensual torment until her head tipped back on his shoulder and her breath was coming out fast and strong. He transferred the glass to his other hand and began the same kneading motion on her right breast. He put the champagne to her lips, smiling as she drank mindlessly while her body writhed to his touch.

By the time the glass was empty, her moans were

loud and her tender peaks were hard like pebbles. He dropped the glass to the carpet and cupped her creamy fullness with both hands, drawing his fingertips together until both her nipples rested between a thumb and forefinger. He pinched, gently.

She screamed, arching her body into his touch.

He rotated the excited flesh, ignoring her pleas to desist, to do it harder, and finally to make love to her. He wanted to draw this out, to give her more pleasure than she could imagine. His own body ached for a release he refused to give it.

"Please, Hakim. Please... Please... Oh, you have to stop. No. Do it harder." Her head thrashed from side to side against his shoulder. "I can't stand it!"

"But you can. Your body is capable of great pleasure." He whispered the words into her ear, knowing the warmth of his breath would add to her passionate enjoyment.

"Then please me," she implored.

Without warning, he dropped one hand down to her thigh and discovered something he had not noticed before. Her gown was slit all the way up her hip. Primitive satisfaction flowed through him as he delved beneath the satin to tangle in the dewy curls at the juncture of her thighs.

"Oh!" She tipped her pelvis toward his hand and his forefinger slipped onto the slick bud of her femininity.

He circled it once. Twice. And she came apart, her scream echoing in the room as her body shuddered in ecstasy against his own. He continued to touch her until she convulsed again and then shook with each light stroke of his finger.

"Oh, Hakim, it's too much." Her tormented whisper came just before her entire body went limp in his arms.

She would have fallen but for the intimate hold he had on her. He just held her, his sex hard and hurting, but the satisfaction in giving her pleasure so deep, he had no real desire to let go.

Her head turned and her lips pressed against his neck. "I love you." Her whisper against his flesh was finally too much for his control.

"I want to make you my wife." Hakim's growl against her temple barely registered in Catherine's pleasure sated state.

But being spun around and kissed to within an inch of her life did.

Unbelievably his passion sparked renewed life in the erogenous centers of her body, causing extremely sensitive nipples to tighten almost painfully and swollen flesh to throb. She opened her lips, wanting his tongue. He did not disappoint her. He conquered her mouth with a sensual invasion that took the strength from her limbs and she sagged against him.

He swept her high against his chest and soon she found herself being lowered to the silk covered bed. Breaking the kiss, he loomed above her, his expression sending jolts of pure adrenalin through her body.

"You belong to me."

Tears of intense emotion burned her eyelids. "Yes."

This time when his lips touched hers, the passion was laced with a sense of purpose. He peeled off the silk robe he'd worn out of the bathroom and laid his completely naked body along hers. Hot satin skin inundated her senses everywhere their bodies collided. She started to tremble as if she'd been playing in the snow too long, uncontrollable shivers of sensation wracking her body.

Her reaction did not seem to concern him. Warm

masculine lips never parted from her own while talented fingers skimmed the sleek smoothness of her nightgown. She felt as if the air she was taking in was devoid of oxygen.

Breaking the kiss, she tossed her head against the pillows. *"Hakim."* She could not form another word, just his name.

He reared up above her, gloriously naked, gloriously male. "It is time."

The words were ominous. Her eyes widened as he leant forward and began the process of pulling her nightgown up her body. She was glad for the subdued lighting as the sudden memory of her physical imperfections rose up to taunt her.

He sensed her miniscule withdrawal immediately. "What is it?"

He'd see soon enough anyway. Perhaps if she told him, the scars would not come as such an unpleasant shock.

"I have marks." She couldn't bring herself to say the ugly word *scars*. "From the summer I grew so fast."

She could tell nothing from his expression as he finished removing her white satin covering. He then did something that took her completely by surprise. He rose, moving until one foot rested on the floor and one knee on the bed. Then he reached out and pulled one of the scarves from a wall sconce increasing the light in the room by almost tenfold.

Flinching, she felt the desire drain from her like water draining from an unplugged cistern to be replaced by dismay.

"Hakim, please..."

But then her gaze settled on his fully naked, fully aroused body and she forgot to worry about his reaction to her scars in the new and more gripping concern over making love for the first time. Was he as big as he looked or was that her inexperience showing? She wasn't about to ask him.

That would be mortifying.

New brides did not ask questions like that of their husbands but she had to.

"Are you oversized, or am I just worried?" The words blurted out of her mouth, halting the tan hand reaching toward her.

His head snapped up and she could tell she'd surprised him. That was fine with her. She'd downright shocked herself. Could she have gotten more gauche?

He gestured with both hands toward his erect flesh, a rueful expression on his face. "I am what I am. I do not measure myself against other men." He sounded deeply offended by the very thought.

Well, good on him, but that didn't answer her question, did it? And anxiety ridden or not, she was beginning to have deep misgivings about proportionate sizes. For the first time since she was ten years old, she felt very small and fragile. It was not an entirely pleasant feeling.

Her gaze skittered to his face. He didn't look like one iota of his desire had deserted him. In fact, he was looking at her like a ravenous wolf ready for its first meal after a long, hungry stretch. The shaking she had experienced earlier came back, but this time it was liberally laced with anxiety.

Despite his apparent hunger, when he touched her it was with a featherlight fingertip.

He brushed along the thin ridge of raised flesh at the juncture between her arm and body, then reached across her and traced the matching one on her other side.

"They are barely an inch long and very narrow. From your concern, I thought they would be much bigger."

"They're ugly."

"No, they are not."

There was no arguing with such an implacable tone and she didn't really want to. Was it possible the blemishes truly didn't bother him?

"I have some on the sides of my knees as well." She never wore short dresses because of them.

His attention was no longer on the old flaw. It had strayed along with his hands to the generous curves of her breasts. She felt them swell and tighten in response and a small moan escaped her. He bent down, lowering his head until she had no doubt of his intention.

Her breath froze in her chest as she waited for the incredible pleasure of his mouth on her. Only when it came, it landed first on one of the scars. His tongue traced where his fingertip had before and her moan this time was much louder. His mouth swiftly braced over her body until he closed it over one now turgid peak and her body involuntarily bowed off the bed, pushing her excited flesh more firmly into his mouth. Her eyes closed on the exquisite pleasure. She cried out when his hands grasped her rib cage, keeping her pressed against his mouth while he kissed, nibbled and sucked in an ever increasing circular pattern over first one breast and then the other. He was very thorough, giving every centimeter of sensitized flesh erotic attention.

He lifted his head and she gasped in protest at the loss of his pleasurable ministrations.

"You said your knees have these small marks as well?"

"What?" She got no further as his fingers began a comprehensive inspection of the area around her knees, pressing her legs apart so he could touch the stretch marks on her inner knees as well.

"I must admit, when I am here, such tiny scratches cannot hold my attention. I find other things of far more interest."

Catherine knew exactly what he meant as his fingertips started a slow glide up her inner thigh and she had to admit her stretch marks had stopped mattering to her with the first stroke of his tongue several minutes ago. Just remembering what it had felt like when he had touched her between her legs before had her aching, burning and squirming against the silk coverlet.

"Hakim?"

"Hmm?" His fingertips were on the hypersensitive flesh just before the juncture to her thighs.

"Could you put the scarf back on the lamp?"

She felt vulnerable, open and naked to his gaze and the harsh light only increased that feeling.

"Is that what you really want?" As he asked the question his fingers trespassed her most intimate flesh, finding tissues wet and swollen in preparation for their joining.

"Oh...my...gosh..." she panted as one masculine digit slid inside her untried body.

He pressed forward until she flinched with pain. He did not draw all the way out, only far enough that the discomfort left. "You are very responsive."

He delighted her too, but she couldn't get the words past the constriction in her throat.

"I want you so very much, but you must be made ready." There was no mistaking the sincerity of his statement. His voice sounded tortured.

"I'm ready now," she fairly screamed as he began

moving that one finger in and out, stretching her, exciting her.

"No, but you will be. It is my responsibility as your husband and your lover to make it so."

She would have answered, but his thumb had found her sweet spot and her vocal chords were only capable of moans.

"There is an ancient tradition among my grandfather's people for the women to prepare the bride for her husband by dispensing with the maidenhead. Thus there is no pain on the wedding night." His deep voice mesmerized her. "However, I must admit to a primitive satisfaction in knowing you have left this privilege to me."

"You're not going to do it so long as it's only your hand on me." It had been a struggle to get the words out.

His laughter was low and rich. "Ah, little kitten, you are so innocent. I could indeed, but I prefer to wait for my complete possession of you."

"Are we—"

The feel of a second finger joining the first inside her cut off the question of whether he intended to wait all night to make that possession.

She felt full and only slightly uncomfortable as he made the same motions with two fingers he had made with one. Tension built inside her, a now recognizable strain toward fulfillment. Just as she felt the precipice near, he withdrew his hand.

Her eyes, which had been closed in ecstatic pleasure, flew open and she looked at him, but all she saw was the top of his head as he did something she was totally unprepared for. As his mouth settled over intimate flesh she instinctively tried to arch away, but strong fingers held her hips in place.

"Hakim. *Oh, Hakim.* Please… Oh, my gosh! It's too much. Don't stop, please don't stop!"

It was unlike anything she'd known, even in his arms. The intimacy of his action mortified her on one level, but the physical sensations more than conquered her mental misgivings.

Pleasure built. Tension increased. Her body strained against his mouth, her hips against his hands. Her mouth opened on a silent scream. She thrashed. Her hands gripped the quilt. Her heels dug into the bed.

All the while, the sensual torment continued.

Then it all coalesced into a crescendo of delight so intense, she screamed wildly with the joy of it.

It was then, at that moment of intense delight that he moved up her body and slid inside her, breaking through her small barrier with a pain she hardly acknowledged. Her body was too busy dealing with the aftermath of what he had just given her.

She looked into his black eyes, her own swimming with tears and said the words she knew he was thinking. "I'm yours now."

"Yes."

She smiled at that one arrogant word. "You're mine too."

"Can you doubt it?"

And he started to move and incredibly it all began again. This time when her body convulsed, his feral shout joined her feminine whimpers as the overwhelming pleasure ignited a crying jag of monumental proportions.

He was no more affected by this than he had been by her shaking earlier. He hugged her close and whispered to her in a mixture of Arabic and English, every word and caress seemed to be assurance and praise for her femininity and passion.

Her tears finally subsided and he carried her to the bathroom where he showered with her, washing her body with meticulous care and then groaning in delight when she insisted on returning the favor.

She discovered that a soapy hand and curiosity could end in a very male satisfaction.

She was still smiling at her own daring and success when they exited the shower and he began drying her with a towel.

"I can do that."

"But it gives me greater pleasure to do it than to watch."

"Are you going to let me dry you?" she asked, grinning cheekily at him.

He laughed out loud. "You are flushed with your triumph in the shower, are you not?"

She felt herself blushing, but nodded. "It's nice knowing you aren't the only one giving the pleasure around here."

He stood up and placed his hands on her shoulders, his expression terribly serious. "The joy your response gives me is greater than any I have ever known."

Her breath caught in her throat. She could definitely get used to the flowery and extravagant way of talking passion seemed to elicit in him. "Thank you."

They went back into the bedroom and he brought forth that same uninhibited response in her three more times before they fell into exhausted slumber, wrapped tightly in one another's arms.

CHAPTER SEVEN

MYRIAD impressions stamped Catherine's awareness through the tinted windows of the stretch limousine on their way from the airport to the Royal Palace of Jawhar. The gray of the window glass muted the harsh light glinting off the desert sand and roads that seemed to stretch into nothingness. Yet Hakim had assured her that they were quite close to the Royal Palace as well as the capital city of Jawhar.

Both would be found on the other side of the tall sand dunes that appeared to swallow the road on which they traveled.

She was grateful for the air-conditioned car as her skin already prickled with the heat of nerves. She would be sweating if the car matched the heated temperatures outside.

Catherine adjusted the long chiffon scarf draped over her hair for the tenth time in as many minutes and the fragrance of jasmine tickled her senses. This time she crossed the filmy fabric at her neck, letting the excess dangle down her back. She was glad women in Jawhar did not wear veils. Hakim had told her she didn't even have to wear the head covering, but she had wanted to out of respect to his uncle. The King.

The car topped the sand dunes and suddenly her vision was filled with the massive domed structure of the Royal Palace.

Hakim had grown up here since the age of ten. He'd shared that bit of information over breakfast, but had not told her why and she hadn't asked, being too awed by the prospect of meeting the rest of the royal family. What if they didn't like her? How could an American woman be their first choice for Sheikh Hakim bin Omar al Kadar? For here, he was a sheikh, not just an extremely wealthy businessman.

And he looked the part. Her gaze strayed momentarily from the rapidly approaching palace to the man she had married less than twenty-four hours ago.

Hakim in full Arab mode was somewhat intimidating. Dressed much as the sheikh in her fantasies, he wore white, loose-fitting pants, a long white tunic over them, and a black *abaya* that looked like a cross between a robe and a cloak over that. His head covering was the only deviation. It was white like his pants and shirt with a gold *egal* holding it in place, the ends of the golden rope twisted and tucked into the band that circled his head.

She'd seen a red and white checkered head covering in his suitcase and couldn't help wondering if he wore it when he was amidst his grandfather's Bedouin tribe.

Her eyes flicked between him and the home of his youth. Even the gray tinting on the windows could not disguise the bright colors of the domes, walls and revealing archways of the huge complex.

Her heart started to hammer.

She was going to meet a king in less than five minutes.

She smoothed a miniscule wrinkle out of the overdress of the caftan ensemble she was wearing. She'd adored it on sight. The underdress was the simplest component. It was floor length and cream in color with wine roses embroidered around the hem and sleeves. The matching overdress had a V-neck outlined in the roses and was sleeveless. Both sides were slit up to her waist for ease of walking, and to expose more of the underdress's fancy work.

It, along with several other gorgeous things to wear while on their honeymoon in his homeland, had been Hakim's gift to her that morning.

She tugged her sleeves so they fell past her wrists.

"If you don't stop fidgeting, your dress will be in tatters by the time we reach my uncle's palace."

She gave Hakim a wry grimace. "I've never met a king before."

"Now you are married to a sheikh. It is expected."

"Have you noticed that since arriving in your country, you've gotten more arrogant?" And that was saying a lot. She thought he'd been pretty imposingly confident before.

He smiled. "Is that so?"

"Even your voice has changed. You've always had a certain air of authority, but since getting off the plane you just exude power."

"I am considered one of the rulers of my country. I am the only remaining sheikh of Kadar."

"I'm surprised your uncle encourages you to live in the States then."

"There are some duties only family can perform."

Those were the last words between them before the limousine slid to a halt outside the Royal Palace of Jawhar.

Hakim helped her from the car, but then removed his hand from her arm and maintained a distance of at least ten inches between them as they made their way inside the palace.

The incredible splendor, vibrant colors and grandiose size surrounding her, registered even as she kept her eyes fixed firmly on the huge wooden double doors they were headed towards. Just before they reached them, a servant wearing a headdress and flowing garments stepped forward to open the one on the right so that she and Hakim could walk through.

If the entranceway had been impressive, the formal reception room was overwhelming. Mosaic patterns interspersed with ornate carpets dyed a predominant red covered the floor that stretched at least fifty feet in each direction. Her eyes only skimmed the furniture and no doubt original statuary surrounding the room, before they settled on the man sitting in a chair that could only be described as a throne on a raised wooden dais.

''Bring your bride forward, Hakim.''

Hakim took her hand then and led her forward until they stood only a foot from his uncle, the King.

The next two hours were a complete haze as she was first presented to King Asad bin Malik al Jawhar and then introduced to Hakim's other relatives on his father's side and expected to converse with them. Where her wedding had been both exciting and terrifying, this was worse. She did not know these people, did not speak their language and every single one of them had their attention fixed firmly on her.

She'd been shy all her life and her first instinct was to hide behind a wall of reserve or a nearby pillar, but she refused to let Hakim down. So, she forced herself to smile and talk to the intimidating strangers.

King Asad came up and hugged Hakim at one point. ''Your duty is more pleasing than you at first expected, hmm?''

''Yes, Uncle. I am content.''

Since both men were looking at her, Catherine assumed the comment was directed to her in some way and felt herself blushing at its implications.

"She is charming." The King's tendency to speak of her as if she wasn't there made her want to smile. He was much more traditionally Arab than Hakim, who had been educated in France and then America. "Her fair skin reveals her blushes and innocence I think."

"Can you doubt it?"

She felt like melting through the floor. They couldn't be discussing what she thought they were discussing, but after the big deal Hakim had made over her virginity she suspected they were. He'd said it was important to his family, she remembered.

"No, I do not doubt it. Assurances were made."

Assurances were made? What the heck did that mean? She wasn't about to ask in front of his uncle, but she was going to find out if Hakim had told the older man that she'd admitted to being a virgin. Just the thought of them talking about her like that made her skin heat with a truly mortified blush.

"*Hakim.*" Her voice came out strangled and not at all *charming*.

Hakim's expression had turned wary, as well it should be. "Yes?"

"If you and your uncle are talking about what I think you are talking about, things could get ugly very quickly."

As threats went, it appeared to be very effective because Hakim excused them on the pretext that she was tired from the long journey.

"Stop by Abdul-Malik's office on your way to your apartments. He has the final geologist's report for you to review before Mr. Benning can begin his excavations."

Catherine stopped walking at the second mention of her father. ''My dad's mining company is coming to Jawhar?''

''Yes.''

''Why didn't you tell me?''

''It is not important to us, unless you wish to visit him when he is here.''

''Yes, women should not concern themselves with business.''

She chose to ignore the king's chauvinistic remark. There were still men among her father's generation who agreed with him, not to mention her own mother's willful ignorance of her father's business dealings.

However, she was determined to discuss the issue with Hakim when they made it to their private apartments.

Hakim's seemingly limitless ardor prevented any conversation but that which occurred between lovers from taking place as he made love to her throughout the lazy warm hours of the afternoon.

Several hours later, she was dressed for their official wedding celebration dinner and waiting for Hakim to finish a business call when she noticed the geologist's report again. She wasn't surprised her father had moved quickly to take advantage of his new connection to Hakim's resource rich, if small country.

She picked up the report, wondering what type of mining her father planned to do here. She didn't recognize the named ore, which was nothing new. Geology had not been one of her strong suits in school. Her interest had always been books and teaching children to appreciate and use them to their advantage.

As she scanned the first page, the date of the initial

inquiry caught her eye. At first she wondered if it had been a typo, but other dates coincided with that being the initial query. The problem was that it was for a date significantly *prior* to her meeting Hakim for the first time at the Whitehaven Library. Her brain scrambled to understand what her eyes were telling her.

Hakim had known her father before they met.

She shook her head. No. This report was for Jawhar. His uncle had surely had business dealings with her father, but that did not mean Hakim had been apprised of them until later.

It seemed like such a huge coincidence though. Why hadn't her father or Hakim mentioned it? He obviously knew now. When had he found out?

The questions were still whirling through her mind when she looked up to find Hakim's gaze locked firmly on her. His face was completely expressionless and for some reason that really worried her.

She laid the report down, feeling an inexplicable need to make sure it lay in the exact spot from which she had originally picked it up. "It's dated for some time before we met."

"That report is confidential." The words were hard, clipped, unlike any tone she'd heard from him before.

"Even from your wife?"

"I do not expect you to concern yourself with my business dealings."

"You sound just like your uncle."

Hakim's head cocked arrogantly in acceptance of that fact.

"I don't believe women are too stupid to understand business dealings and you'd better accept that I'm not going to pretend ignorance to feed your male ego."

That made his eyes narrow, but she ignored the reaction.

"Why didn't you tell me you had met my dad?" She made the accusation as a wild stab in the dark, hoping he would deny it. She wanted to believe the original business had been conducted between his uncle and her father.

"Harold thought it would be best."

A mixture of raw emotions swirled through her, but chief among them was confusion. Why would her father suggest keeping their business dealings a secret from her? "Did he think I might reject you once I knew you two were business associates?"

"I believe that was his concern, yes. You had shown that marked tendency for the past several years."

"But *you* had to know my feelings for you were genuine, that I wouldn't turn away from our relationship just because you and my father knew each other." She felt like she was navigating her way through heavy fog without the aid of headlamps.

"It was not a risk I was willing to take."

Because he was falling in love with her and hadn't wanted to risk losing her? For a guy with Hakim's arrogance, such an explanation just did not ring true, no matter how much her whimpering heart wanted it to.

She tried to make sense of everything while her husband watched her, his expression wary. Hakim had known her father before meeting her at the library.

"My father set us up."

Something flickered in his eyes and she had the strangest sense he was going to lie to her.

"If you won't tell me the truth, then don't say anything at all."

He jolted, his black eyes widening fractionally before

the emotional mask once again fell into place. "Not all truth is desirable."

"I don't care. I won't be lied to by my husband."

"Your father arranged for us to meet, yes." The words came out grimly and gave no satisfaction at all.

He was right, some truth was unpalatable.

As unpalatable as having her virginity discussed between her husband and his uncle. Almost as if she were watching a movie screen, the scene in the reception room played over in her mind.

His uncle, looking pompous with a bearded face and white robes of state. *Her fair skin reveals her blushes and innocence I think.*

Hakim's expression sardonic. *Can you doubt it?*

Herself standing there, blushing painfully.

The King taking a deep breath and letting it out with an expression of supreme complacency. *No, I do not doubt it. Assurances were made.*

And suddenly she understood what assurances had been made and by who. "You asked my father if I was a virgin before you asked me to marry you!"

In a very peripheral way, she realized she was yelling. She never yelled. She was the quiet one, the one who stayed in the shadows and was content to do so, but she didn't feel like being quiet. She felt like screaming the place down.

"He volunteered the information."

"Is that supposed to make me feel better?" Why in the world would her dad have felt the need to tell Hakim she'd never had a serious boyfriend? "It's not like you couldn't have made an educated guess on your own."

Her lack of experience around men had to have been obvious.

"I did not know you then."

"Are you telling me that you discussed my virginity with my father before we ever met?" Dread was curling its ugly tentacles around her heart even as she hoped against hope that he would deny the charge.

Hakim's eyes closed as if he was seeking an answer and then he opened them and jet black glittered at her with hard purpose. "This is not something you truly wish to know. It will only upset you to discuss this further and it will serve no good purpose. We are married. That is all that matters now."

No way. "My being able to trust my husband matters."

He drew himself up, his expression going grim. "You have no reason to mistrust me."

"If you've lied to me, I do."

"There is a proverb among my people. *Lying in its proper place is equal to worship.*"

She felt the words like a slap. Was he admitting to lying to her? "Well, there is a proverb among my people. A lying tongue hides a lying heart."

"Your father and my uncle discussed your innocence prior to our meeting the first time." He bit the words out. "Does that please you to know?" The sarcasm hurt.

"You know it doesn't." She wasn't yelling anymore. In fact, she could barely get more than a whisper past the tears now aching for release. "I was just a pity date."

And not even a pity date arranged between her father and Hakim, but one arranged between two old men. Had she not been a virgin, she had the awful feeling even a pity date would not have occurred. It was medieval and felt like the worst kind of betrayal.

"Why didn't you tell me?"

He reached out, following her when she backed up and took both her shoulders in a gentle but firm grip. His thumbs rubbed against her collarbones. "You are my wife. Does the reason we met mean so much?"

Of course it mattered, her mind screamed. "He fixed us. He even told you I was a virgin! *You don't think that matters?*" she asked, trying not to choke on the words.

"Are you saying you would have been content to give your innocence to another?"

How dare he sound offended?

"Stop trying to sidetrack the issue! You lied to me. My father lied to me. I feel manipulated and it hurts, Hakim. It hurts more than you can imagine."

"It was a lie of omission only." His hands moved to cup her face. "Was this so terrible? If I had told you the truth, you would have rejected me like you rejected all the others. We would not be married now. Is that what you want?"

He wasn't putting it back on her like that. She yanked her face from his grasp. "I love you. I wouldn't have rejected you because of the truth."

"Like you are not rejecting me now?"

"I'm not rejecting you," she screamed, out of control and in emotional pain, "I'm rejecting being lied to, being betrayed by the man I love."

How could he not understand that? "How would you like knowing I had colluded with your family behind your back? How would you like knowing you'd been made a total fool of?"

"How did we make a fool of you? Do you consider it folly to have married me?"

They stood facing each other, two combatants on a battlefield of emotional carnage.

Her shoulders slumped, all energy draining from her as she acknowledged the truth that came from knowing he had been dishonest with her. "Yes, if it meant tying myself to a man I cannot trust."

"You are making more of this than it is," he retorted coolly.

"Am I?" Two words whispered so low, she didn't know if he heard them, but he moved.

"Yes."

She shook her head. Denial? Confusion? She didn't know, but it served to loosen the hot wetness gritting behind her eyes. He pulled her into his body again as she started to cry, great gulping sobs that sounded as awful as they felt. She struggled, but he was too strong and she gave in, letting the grief take over. He didn't try to quiet her, but just held her, seeming to realize she had to have this emotional outburst.

Eventually the tears subsided and he handed her a handkerchief to mop herself up. She stepped away from him to do so.

He watched her broodingly. "How we came together is no longer important. You must believe this. We are husband and wife. Your father's interference has no bearing on our future. We make of our marriage what we choose to make of it."

The crying had calmed her enough to really take in what he was saying and his words made her stop and think.

She'd been rebelling against her dad's interference in her life since reaching adulthood, but could she really regret meeting Hakim just because Harold Benning had a hand in it? Or even his uncle for that matter? Two old men had played matchmaker and discussed private affairs of hers they had no business discussing, but in the end she had married the man she loved. No one had coerced her.

Unlike the other men her father had fixed her up with, Hakim didn't need anything from Harold Benning.

No matter what had brought them together, he had married her for her own sake and he loved her. But a man who loved her would not have lied to her, would he?

"It hurts that you hid this from me, that you didn't trust my love enough to believe I wouldn't let it matter. A-And…a lie by omission is still a lie." She was trying not to cry again and her words came out stuttered.

"It was not my intention to hurt you."

"But you did."

"This I can see. I made a mistake." She could sense this was not easy for him to admit.

"You didn't trust my love."

"I did not see it that way."

If he hadn't seen it that way, then, "Why did you lie to me?"

"It was your father's wish."

It was chauvinism at its worse for her dad to think he had the right to ask Hakim to keep the secret and for Hakim to believe he had an obligation to do so. Maybe how they met wasn't so important, but where she stood in his list of priorities was. So was knowing he would never lie to her again.

"My wishes should come first with you. I'm your wife and you made promises to love and cherish me. My father has no place in our relationship."

"That is what I have been saying."

"Then promise me that from now on I come first in your considerations." She meant between her and her father. She knew she could not come first over everything for a man in Hakim's position.

"This I will do."

"Do you *promise*?" He always kept his promises.

He brushed the wetness from under her eyes with his thumbs. "I promise."

"You're big on keeping your promises. I remember you telling me that."

"This is true."

"Then promise me one more thing."

He looked wary. "What?"

"That you will never lie to me again."

He hesitated and she glared at him. "I don't care if you think the truth will upset me. I can't trust you if I believe you'll lie to me, even if it is to protect my feelings."

"Then I promise this also."

She nodded, feeling a sense of relief that he had agreed so easily. If she couldn't trust him, she could not stay with him, no matter how much she loved him. "I need to fix my makeup."

He drew her forward and dropped a soft kiss on her lips. It felt like an apology and she took it as such.

He released her. "Be quick. The dinner will have started without the guests of honor."

CHAPTER EIGHT

LATER, sitting between her husband and the wife of one of his cousins, she thought the dinner would go on forever. It wasn't that the company was not entertaining. They were. Hakim's cousin's wife was sweet and everyone had been very kind to Catherine, but her husband was driving her crazy.

He seemed to have gotten it in his head that she needed reassurance regarding their marriage. Physical reassurance.

Since it was considered unseemly among his people for a husband and wife to touch in public, all of his touches were surreptitious. And dangerous. Under the cover of the table, he caressed her thigh through the black lace overlay of her dress.

He had told her to dress in Western style for the dinner. She'd been glad she'd followed his advice when she arrived to find the other women similarly attired, although the men wore traditional Arab costume.

However, when she felt Hakim's foot brush the inside of her calf under her long skirt, she wished she was wearing more than a pair of sheer stockings. Her body was humming with the excitement only he could generate and no way to appease it. They could not leave the dinner until his uncle excused them.

She turned her head to tell him to stop it and found herself mesmerized by a pair of obsidian eyes.

"Hakim."

99

"Yes, *aziz*?" His foot moved and sensation arced right up her leg to the very core of her.

She gasped.

He smiled.

She was still smarting a little from their earlier argument, but he had promised never to lie to her again. "If you don't stop it my foot is going to make contact with your leg as well, but it will still have a shoe on and its sharp toe will be the point of impact."

He laughed and popped a grape into her mouth. "Your impact on my body is sharp indeed."

She couldn't help smiling at him.

He removed his foot and winked.

She sighed with exasperation and turned to her other dinner companion, Lila.

The other woman turned to her and smiled warmly. "You and Sheikh Hakim are well matched."

"Thank you."

"It is good to see him find pleasure in a duty that must have been hard to accept."

"Yes." The more time she spent around Hakim in Jawhar, the more she realized how much he had sacrificed of his personal happiness to oversee the family's business interests abroad.

"In my opinion, it was not necessary. It seems reactionary to believe the dissidents could force the family into fleeing the country. And, after all, marriage to an American would be difficult for the more traditional members of our family, but Hakim is content." Lila leaned forward and whispered, "My husband would never approve my having a career."

Considering the fact the woman's husband was the Crown Prince of Jawhar, even Catherine could understand his reasoning. Being a queen would be a full-time job.

Catherine didn't know what her marriage had to do with politics. "Does King Asad really believe a coup could succeed?"

"I do not think so. I believe he assigned Sheikh Hakim his duty to be prepared in case it is so, but not out of real necessity. The dissidents have less support than they did twenty years ago and that uprising failed."

"It's too bad the king will not trust anyone but family to oversee the business interests. Hakim would be happier living here in Jawhar." Catherine was certain of it.

"Perhaps my honored father-in-law could be persuaded to assign a trusted advisor to oversee the business affairs for the family, but he would only trust family to fulfill the duty assigned to Hakim."

Catherine didn't understand. Was the language barrier the problem, or was Lila implying that Hakim had additional duties in the States?

"After all, only a family member could be trusted to sponsor the others for living visas in the United States. I think your government may even require it to be a relation. You would know better than I."

Catherine's confusion at finding the date on the geologist's report was nothing compared to what she felt now. "I don't understand," she admitted.

Lila smiled. "I found it rather complicated when my husband told me about it as well. It pleases me that he shares so much with me. In some ways he is very traditional, but he does not dismiss my intellect."

Catherine would have felt more empathy if she wasn't so puzzled. "Can you explain it to me?"

"Why don't you ask Hakim? I, too, prefer not to

admit to my husband when I don't understand something he has explained. I suppose it is an issue of pride." She sighed, then smiled. "It's quite simple, really. Once Hakim married you, he was then eligible through you to sponsor long-term living visas for members of his family provided he could guarantee their income. Which, of course is no problem."

"Long-term living visas?" Catherine choked out.

Lila nodded and went on. "Then of course there is the mining partnership. King Asad wants to realize the benefit of the geologist's findings. He is convinced your father's company is key to making that happen."

"Mining partnership?" Catherine asked, her voice faint to her own ears.

Lila missed the question and leaned forward confidingly. "My husband thought King Asad would surely bring forth a more distant relation for the marriage alliance until he realized that as usual, his father had other benefits in mind."

"Long-term living visas." The words came out of her subconscious as Catherine dealt on a conscious level with the other things Lila had told her.

Lila nodded. "King Asad is a sharp negotiator."

Catherine's mind was still stuck on the concept that a marriage had been part of the mining deal. *Her marriage?* "You mean Hakim's duty was to marry me?" Catherine whispered in dawning horror.

Lila's brow furrowed. "Well, yes. You could put it like that."

Catherine wondered if there was any other way of putting it. "The further benefits of my marriage to your husband's cousin were the long-term living visas in case political dissidents made them necessary?" she asked, clarifying it in her mind as she spoke.

This time Lila did not answer, seeming to finally latch onto the fact that what she'd been saying was news to Catherine. And not welcome news.

For her part, Catherine was finding it almost impossible to wrap her mind around the idea that her marriage had been arranged as part of a business deal with Benning Excavations. That the man she believed had loved her had lied to her and tricked her. No love there.

Lila looked worried. Really worried.

Catherine felt sick to her stomach and had to swallow down bile as her throat convulsed. Everyone at the dinner probably knew that she was the albatross around Hakim's neck. Necessary for him to fulfill his duty, but *not* a wife he truly wanted and desired. Certainly not a loved wife.

Humiliation lanced through like a jagged edged sword.

"Does the whole family know?" she asked, needing confirmation of the worst.

Lila shook her head vehemently. "No one outside of King Asad, Abdul-Malik, my husband, Hakim and you know of the plan."

Learning that the mortifying truth was known by only a select few did not lessen the pain threatening to engulf her in a tide of black anguish. She'd been betrayed on every level. Her father had lied to her. Her husband had lied to her. She'd been used as a means to an end by a king she'd never even met before today.

She'd been used to fulfill his duty by the man seated next to her. The swine. The no good, double-dealing… She couldn't think of a word bad enough to describe him.

She hated him.

She hated herself more. She'd been such a fool.

Twenty-four-years old and still too stupid to realize when she was being manipulated and used. Hakim did not love her. He didn't even care about her. You didn't use people you cared about. What did that say about her dad?

She felt another wave of sickness wash over her.

Did her mother know?

Did Felicity? No. Felicity would have told her.

"Are you all right? You've turned very pale." Lila's concerned voice barely penetrated the fog of pain surrounding Catherine.

Lila leaned around Catherine. "Sheikh Hakim. I think your wife is ill."

Hakim turned, his duplicitous face cast in a false show of concern. "Is something wrong?"

"You don't have a heart." Venom born from an unbearable pain laced each word. "I hate you."

He reeled back as if she had struck him. Lila's shocked gasp barely registered. Catherine just wanted out of there. She was breaking up, her heart shattering into jagged pieces inside her chest. She went to stand, but Hakim caught her and held her to her chair.

"What is going on?"

"Let me go."

"No. Explain what has you so upset."

"You lied to me."

"We discussed this. You understood." Even now, he wasn't going to admit the full truth.

"I'm the duty. You *had* to marry me." Her voice rose with each successive word until she was practically shouting. "It was part of some mining deal with my father!"

Hakim's gaze slid to Lila. "What did you tell her?"

Catherine answered for the other woman. "She told

me the truth, something my husband and father did not see fit to do.''

She could hear King Asad inquiring about what the problem was. Her husband's answer and his anger both registered in the peripheral of her consciousness. As did Lila's profuse apologies. It was all there, but none of it was real. She couldn't take it in.

She'd felt the pain of rejection many times in her life, but nothing had ever been like this. To know she was nothing more than a commodity to be bartered by her dad and a means to an end to the man she had loved. To know where she had believed herself loved, she had been merely tolerated. It was too much. Too much betrayal. Too much pain to take in.

She tried to stand again, forgetting Hakim's iron grip on her arm. She looked at his hand curled around the black lace sleeve. It hurt to see it, to know he was touching her. She didn't want his hand on her, but her voice would not work to tell him so. So, she looked away, letting her gaze roam over the rest of the room.

Shockingly no one seemed to notice the holocaust of emotion at the head table.

Then she realized that everyone else had kept their voices down, their expressions bland. Even Lila, whose eyes registered remorse wore a plastic smile on her lips. Hakim was no longer talking to King Asad.

He was talking to her, but the words weren't registering over the rushing in her ears.

''I want to go to our room,'' she said, right over the words coming out of her husband's mouth. ''Please tell your uncle I am not feeling well and must go.''

She wondered if he would argue with her.

He didn't.

She watched dispassionately as he turned to his uncle,

spoke a few words in the other man's ear and then turned back to her.

"He will give his official blessing to our marriage and then we will be free to go."

She did not respond.

She simply sat, wishing Hakim would let go of her arm, while the King stood and spoke his official blessing. When he was done, he instructed the newlyweds to retire to their apartments, saying they had better things to do than listen to old men tell jokes well into the night. The room exploded in laughter, but Catherine's sense of humor had vanished.

Hakim pulled her to her feet.

She swayed. Stupid. She refused to let her body be so affected by her emotional devastation. That is what she told her mind, but the woozy feeling persisted.

Suddenly Hakim swept her into his arms, making a comment about following western tradition and carrying his bride over the threshold. That was supposed to happen in their new home, but she didn't correct him. She doubted anyone cared.

They were all too busy cheering her bastard of a husband's seemingly romantic action.

She said nothing all the way down the long hallway, up the ornate staircase, down another hallway and through the door into their apartments. Silence continued to reign as he released her to sit on the gold velvet covered sofa, but when he went to sit beside her, she spoke.

"I don't want you near me."

He ripped his headgear off and tossed it on the desk. It landed smack on the offending mining report.

"What has changed, Catherine? I have not changed. Our marriage has not changed. We discussed this before the dinner. How we met is not important to our future. It is already in the past.''

She glared at him, wishing looks really could singe.

He sighed heavily. ''There is no need for you to be so upset.''

''No way did you just say that.''

His jaw went taut, his expression frustrated.

''I find out that I've been manipulated by people I should have been able to trust above anyone else in my life, my husband and my father, and you don't think I should be upset?''

He'd grown up in Jawhar, not another planet...even if he was a sheikh. He couldn't be so dense.

''I did not manipulate you.''

''How can you say that?''

''Did I coerce you into marriage?''

''You tricked me.''

''How did I trick you?''

''Are you kidding?'' She threw her hands in the air and even that hurt, like her muscles were as bruised as her emotions. ''You made me believe you were marrying me because you *wanted* to marry me. Whereas in reality it was all some plan your uncle had cooked up with my father.'' Her jaw ached from biting back the tears. ''I thought you loved me.''

''I never said I loved you.''

Her heart felt like it shattered in her chest. ''No. You didn't, but you knew I believed it was me you wanted.''

''I did want to marry you, Catherine.''

''Because it fulfilled your duty to your uncle and because my father made it part of his filthy mining deal with an opportunistic king.''

Hakim tunneled his fingers through his hair and

clasped the back of his neck. "It also fulfilled my desire, little kitten."

"Don't call me that! It doesn't mean anything to you. All those endearments you use. They're just words to you. I thought they were more, but they aren't."

He crossed to her in two strides and fell on his knees before her. "Stop this. You are tearing yourself apart, imagining the worst and it is not true. It pleased me to make you my wife. It pleased you to marry me. Can you not remember that and forget the rest?"

Ebony eyes compelled her to agree.

She wanted to, if only to stop the drumbeat of pain remorselessly pulsing through her. She tried to stifle a whimper, but the broken sound escaped her.

He groaned and pulled her to him. "Why I asked you to marry me is unimportant," he said, speaking into her hair. "The only thing that matters now is that we are married. We can be very happy together."

He was wrong. So wrong. "It is important."

"No." His hand brushed her back. "Many marriages are arranged among my people and they are very happy. It is what we give to our marriage that will determine what it becomes for us. Trust me, jewel of my heart."

She'd been listening right up to that moment, wondering if he was right. Wishing it could be so, but it couldn't.

"I can't trust you." And she wasn't the jewel of his heart. He didn't love her, therefore she had no place in his heart. Rage borne of betrayal welled up in her. She pushed on his chest. *"Get away from me!"*

Again he had that look like she'd smacked him. "I am your husband. You will not speak to me like that."

His arrogance wasn't in the least attractive at that moment.

"You're only my husband until I get home and file for divorce." What that wouldn't do to all his uncle's and her father's machinations.

She supposed that none of them had taken into account the possibility that the worm would turn. They probably thought that she'd stay married to a man who had lied to her and manipulated her. After all, what else did she have to look forward to?

She might not be the kind of woman who haunted men's dreams, but that didn't mean she was willing to live the nightmare of loving someone whose whole purpose in pursuing her had been to use her.

He jumped to his feet and towered over her. "You do not mean that. I will not allow it."

"I don't know how things work in Jawhar," she said with dripping sarcasm, her heart hemorrhaging with grief, "but back home I can file for divorce without the approval of my sheikh husband." Or her deceiving father for that matter.

"You are tired. You are not thinking rationally." He rolled his shoulders as if trying to lessen the tension surrounding them.

She could have told him it wouldn't work. Nothing would work. The tension was born of anguish and it was anguish that had no respite.

"You're wrong. I'm thinking more rationally than I have for the past six weeks."

He shook his head, as if he could negate her words. "You need rest. We will not discuss this further right now."

She crossed her arms over her chest. Was he for real? Okay, maybe that was the way things worked in Jawhar, though she took leave to doubt it. But he'd gone to school in both France and America, both countries hotbeds of feminism. And although she had never considered herself a raving feminist, that didn't mean she was going to let her husband treat her like a child.

"*That's it?* You say we aren't going to talk about it and I'm supposed to shut up and go to bed?"

He rubbed his hand over his face. "That is not what I meant, Catherine. If it pleases you, I am tired, as well. I would be most grateful if we could wait to discuss this further until we have both had a chance to sleep."

As hard as she tried, she could not detect a single note of sarcasm or condensation in his voice. He looked tired, too. Considering how little sleep they'd had the night before and the way they had spent the afternoon, she could even understand why.

But a cynical doubt needled her already agitated brain. Was he just trying to take their battle to a location he had shown his mastery in so well already?

If he was, he had a rude shock coming.

"You're right. I am tired." And heartsick. "I would like to go to bed."

He looked relieved.

"But there is no way on this earth I'm sleeping with you." She said each word as it were its own sentence, spacing them succinctly so there could be no confusion about her intentions.

"You are my wife."

She didn't feel like a wife right now. She felt like a dupe. "I'm your means to an end," she derided.

His body tightened and he pulled himself to his full height, his chilling expression of outrage making him look bigger than his already tall six feet two inches.

"You are my wife," he gritted out between clenched teeth, more angry than she had ever seen him. "Several hundred guests bear witness that this is so. I have legal documents that state you are no longer Miss Catherine Benning, but Catherine bin Hakim al Kadar. Do not ever again say you are not my wife or attempt to deny my name.''

His vehemence shocked her. He looked ready to spit nails. Good. She shouldn't be the only one hurting here. Though, she doubted sincerely he was hurting. Angry more like. Apparently it offended his male ego in a very big way for her to deny the reality of their marriage.

''Legal documents don't make a marriage. They're just paper. They don't prove anything.'' Even in her anger, she doubted her own words. Being married meant something, but not the same thing to her and Hakim evidently.

''The consummation of our marriage is a fact.''

She went hot then cold as his words sank in. ''Are you saying you only made love to me so that I would consider myself married to you?'' she asked wildly, realizing that she was fast approaching the irrational state he'd accused her of earlier. If she wasn't already there.

The question seemed to stun him because his head jerked back and then he stared at her with incredulity in every line of his face. ''You dare ask me such a question?''

''Why not? You married me for reasons I knew nothing about. As far as I'm concerned, all your motives are suspect.''

She watched in a furious kind of fascination as he visibly took control of his anger until his face was a blank mask.

He spun away from her, his hands fisted at his sides the only indication that his emotions were not completely controlled. ''Very well. I will sleep on the divan in here.''

Even in the agony of her devastation, practical considerations asserted themselves. He was way too tall for the smallish divan.

"You can have the bed. I'll sleep out here." She sincerely doubted she'd get much rest anyway.

"Either we share the bed or you sleep in it alone." He still hadn't turned back to face her, but from the sound of his voice, she didn't doubt he meant what he said.

"Fine." If he wanted to suffer, let him suffer. She'd offered a better solution. It was his own fault he was too stubborn to take it, but why he had refused to take it niggled at her conscience. "I'll sleep alone."

A slight inclination of his head was the only indication he had heard her words.

She got up and went into the bedroom. She stopped at the doorway and compulsively looked back at Hakim. There was something incredibly lonely about his stance by the window. He looked as isolated as she felt.

But he'd chosen this path, her mind cried. She hadn't. It had been chosen for her by men who thought she was unworthy of truth and honest consideration. Unworthy of love.

CHAPTER NINE

CATHERINE woke to the smell of coffee.

Her eyelids fluttered, but did not open.

"Good morning. I have brought you breakfast."

The sound of Hakim's voice was a welcome intruder into her slumber until the pain she had escaped for a few short hours in unconsciousness rushed back in a wave so strong she actually moaned.

Masculine fingers tunneled through her hair to cup her scalp. "Are you all right, little kitten?"

The shock of the stupidity of the question brought her eyes wide open and her gaze to the source of her torment.

He was sitting beside her on the bed, wearing a *thob*, but clearly having just woken himself. His hair was mussed, his jaw darkened with morning stubble, his eyes faintly shadowed from what must have been a near sleepless night for him as well. She'd known the divan was too short for him.

How could a man look so very masculine and appealing in something that could be mistaken for full-length robe or dress? Yet, he did. The typical Arabic lounging garment accentuated Hakim's maleness rather than detracting from it. And she didn't want him looking attractive.

She'd come to some very difficult decisions in the long hours of the night. Being reminded of just what she was giving up did not help her resolve or lessen the ache in her heart.

113

Determined to ignore his blatant maleness, she struggled into a sitting position. She tucked the blankets around her, covering the sheer fabric of her nightgown. She didn't want Hakim thinking she was extending any invitations.

His brows rose at the gesture, but he said nothing and laid the rattan breakfast tray across her lap.

There were two croissants on the plate and two demitasse cups of dark, fragrant coffee as well as a small bowl of figs.

She picked up one of the cups of coffee. "Thank you."

"It is my pleasure."

Seeing no reason to put off telling him of her decision, she dove straight in. "I want to go back to Seattle."

He waited to answer until he had finished chewing a bite of his croissant. "We will, inevitably return as planned. My business is there, your job as well."

She placed her cup carefully back on its small white saucer. "I meant today."

The ridge of his jaw became more pronounced. "That is not possible."

"Your jet is broken?"

Rather than respond to the sarcasm in her question, he answered it as if it had not been rhetorical. "No."

"Then I don't see the problem."

"Do you not?" The silky menace in his tone reminded her that this was a man who had been trained since birth to exercise a great deal of authority.

Still, "No," she insisted stubbornly.

"Have you forgotten the wedding ceremony among my grandfather's people?" He asked the question conversationally, as if they were discussing their social schedule rather than the end of one of the shortest marriages on record.

She wasn't about to play the hypocrite. "It would be ridiculous to go through yet another wedding ceremony when I intend to go home and file for divorce, don't you think?"

That elicited a reaction, albeit a subtle one. His entire body tensed as if prepared for battle. "There will be no divorce." So decreed Sheikh Hakim bin Omar al Kadar.

"I don't see how you can stop me." She wasn't one of his subjects.

The expression on his face said she didn't have a very efficient imagination and as much as it shamed her, she shivered. "I mean it, Hakim. I won't stay married to a man who sees me as nothing more than a convenient means to an end."

"You are not a convenience. You are my wife."

"So, you keep saying. Funny, I don't feel like a wife."

Something feral moved in his eyes. "I can take care of that small problem."

She knew just what he meant and she shook her head vehemently. "I'm not going there again."

"Where?" he asked in a honeyed drawl that made her wish she was fully dressed and sitting across a table from him, not a small breakfast tray.

Nevertheless, she refused to let him see how intimidated she felt. "Bed," she said bluntly.

"But we are very compatible in bed." His fingers brushed down the curve of her breast.

She sucked in air, but it didn't help the goose bumps instantly forming on her flesh or the tightening of two erogenous bumps she hoped did not show through the blankets. Her heart felt dead inside her, why didn't her body follow suit?

"That's sex and I'm sure you've been *compatible* with other women before."

"Never like with you."

She wished she could believe him. It would have been some small assuagement for her lacerated pride. But after yesterday, she didn't trust anything he said. "Tell it to the marines."

He laughed at that, though it was a harsh sound. "I have no interest in making love to anyone but you."

"It's not making love when you don't love me."

His superior smile made her want to scream. "Then what is it?"

"Sex, or if you'd rather…" She said a blunt Anglo-Saxon term she had never used before in her life. Then she picked up her croissant and forced herself to take a bite to show she wasn't affected by the conversation.

"Crudeness is unbecoming in you."

She finished chewing her food before speaking. "I'm not interested in what you find becoming. Not anymore."

With a gesture of frustration, he stood up. "Enough."

She glared at him. "You can't order me around like a child."

"Why not? You are behaving like one."

"In what way am I acting childishly?" she demanded.

"You are happy married to me. You love me, yet you threaten to dissolve our marriage on the flimsiest pretext."

"I do not consider betrayal a flimsy excuse!"

"I did not betray you!"

She'd never heard him shout before. She didn't like it.

He took a visible hold on his temper. "When we married, you were so filled with joy, you glowed."

She opened her mouth, but he held his hand up.

"Do not deny it."

"I wasn't going to."

"Good. Finally, we move forward."

"I'm not happy *now*."

"That is apparent, but not something that cannot be changed."

"It will never change," she said with all the despair eating away at her emotions. She'd been happy because she believed the man she loved also loved her. He didn't. End of joy.

He shook his head, the movement decisive. "This I do not believe."

"It may come as a shock to you, but being used by both my father and my husband does not make me happy and since that reality cannot be altered, I don't know how you expect my feelings to change."

Time was supposed to heal all wounds, or so the old saying went, but right at that moment the future stretched forth in one bleak ribbon of pain.

"It is not a matter of being used. I know you resent your father's interference in your life. You have said so, but it is a father's prerogative to find a suitable husband for his daughter. And all the pleasure we found in one another's company awaits only your acceptance of the truth."

"Sex without love is degrading and a father concerned for his daughter's well-being does not sell her in exchange for a mining partnership."

"He did not sell you."

Tears that should be impossible considering how many she had shed in her lonely bed the night before welled and spilled down her cheeks. "Yes, he did. I'm nothing more than a duty wife, bought and paid for."

It hurt so much, she felt as if her heart was being squeezed by a vice.

She turned her face away, not wanting him to witness her grief.

The tray was lifted off her lap. A moment later, she was being pulled into his strength. "Don't cry. Please."

She didn't want him to comfort her. He was the enemy, but there was no one else and the pain was just too heavy to bear alone. His hands rubbed her back, his mouth whispered soothing words while she wept silent tears, soaking the front of his *thob*.

"You are more than a duty wife."

"You don't love me." Her voice broke on each word as the tears competed with her mind for control of her tongue. "You married me because your uncle told you to."

His arms tightened around her, but he did not deny it.

She pressed her face into his chest, wanting to blot out reality. But reality would not be ignored. She was only putting off the inevitable, she realized, allowing Hakim to hold her because she knew it was the last time.

Taking a deep breath, she hiccupped on a sob, but eventually managed to gain control of herself again. She pushed herself from his arms. "I need to get up."

He frowned. "This conversation is not finished."

"I need to get ready to travel."

He searched her face, but she refused to meet his gaze.

Finally, he sighed. "You are right. We need to prepare for our journey to Kadar. We go by helicopter. As much as it pains me to see your hair bound, you should braid it."

Hadn't he heard a word she had said? "I'm not going with you to the desert. I'm going home," she spelled it out as if to a slow-witted child.

"You are wrong." His expression was carved in granite. "You will come with me to *our* home in the desert."

"I won't."

"You will." Standing beside the bed, he looked every inch the Arab prince, his belief in his own authority absolute.

"You can't make me."

"Can I not?"

Frissons of unease shivered along her spine, but she defied him with her eyes. "I'm not going through a second sham of a marriage."

"There is nothing fake about our marriage."

"That's your opinion and you are entitled to it, but it won't change mine."

"I have had enough of this. We will participate in the Bedouin ceremony tomorrow as planned. I will not allow my grandfather to be shamed before his people. Nor will I allow you to dismiss our marriage."

With that, her even-tempered, civilized husband stormed out of the room.

Two hours later, Catherine was dressed in a sleeveless fawn sweater and doeskin pants for traveling. It had a matching calf-length cardigan that made it perfect for the transition in weather from Jawhar to Seattle. And she was going to Seattle, regardless of what her arrogant, deceitful wretch of a husband had decreed.

She checked to make sure her passport was still in her handbag and nodded in satisfaction at the sight of the small blue book. She had cash, her credit cards, everything she needed for departure from Jawhar.

She'd called the airport minutes after Hakim had stormed from their apartments that morning. Then she'd called for a car, reasoning that he was too arrogant to have put a moratorium on her going anywhere. She'd been right. There'd been no problem ordering a car to take her to the airport.

Hakim had assumed she'd wait for him.

That they would continue discussing their marriage.

But there was nothing left to discuss.

She hurt in ways she hadn't known it was possible to hurt and she was not sticking around for more of the same.

She'd come out onto the balcony to wait for a servant to announce her car was ready.

The sights and sounds of Jawhar's capital were open to her as their apartments were on the outer wall of the Royal Palace. While the city was much smaller than Seattle, the cacophonous mixture of voices, beeping horns and tinkling bells that rose to her was more impacting on her senses than Seattle's downtown district. The sun beat against her skin, warming her body while leaving her heart a cold lump in her chest.

A sound in the sitting room alerted her to a servant's arrival.

The trip to the airport was uneventful.

As a member of the royal family, getting a seat on the next flight to a major airline hub was a cinch and within short order she found herself in a first class seat waiting for the plane to take off.

The door closed and then the pilot announced their departure. They taxied to the runway and then stopped, no doubt waiting in line for their takeoff slot.

It seemed a long time coming and other passengers began talking amongst themselves, asking the flight attendant about the delay. Unfortunately, the conversations were in Arabic and she had not yet learned enough to interpret them fully.

But as the minutes ticked on a premonition of dread began to assail her.

When the outer door opened, she watched with almost fatalistic detachment as her husband's form came into view.

His eyes caught hers immediately and the rage she saw in the black depths made her mouth go dry.

He didn't bother to come to her row, but barked out a command to the flight attendant who quickly removed Catherine's bag from the overhead compartment.

Catherine didn't move, but glared her defiance at him.

He could take her bag. She didn't care. She wasn't getting off this plane. "I'm going home."

Hakim did not respond. He spoke again to the flight attendant, this time his voice not so harsh, but the implacability of his tone was apparent even to Catherine, who could not understand what was said.

The flight attendant approached Catherine. "His highness has decreed we cannot take off until you leave the plane, madam."

She didn't need the immediate and quickly escalating grumbling to tell her defeat was staring her in the face. She could not hold everyone back. There was no doubt but that Hakim had the power to ground their plane indefinitely and the hard-faced stranger standing by the open doorway would do it.

She unbuckled her seat and stood up. Hakim turned and left. She followed him off the aircraft, stepping gingerly down the portable stairway that had been transported to the runway for her husband, the sheikh's benefit.

When she reached the bottom, one of the black clad security men led her to a waiting limo.

She climbed into the back seat. She refused to look at her husband. She was both furious and frightened. The level of power he exerted was nothing short of intimidating when she faced the prospect of bucking his will.

Stupid tears burned her throat, but she would not give in to them. Not again.

She'd cried more in the last two days than she had for the past ten years.

Silence reigned for the brief trip in the car.

It stopped and another black clad gentleman opened the door. Hakim climbed out first and then extended his hand to help her out. She ignored it and ignored him.

"You can walk, or I can carry you, but you will come."

"Go to hell." She'd never cursed like that at someone, but she wasn't meekly following Hakim. No way.

A discussion ensued outside the limo.

Then Hakim leaned in, his intent obvious.

She shot to the other side and threw open the door. She scrambled outside only to be caught by manacle-like hands.

"Let me go!" She struggled against the hands and

aimed a kick to her captor's testicles. It never connected.

She was bodily lifted from behind and two arms like steel bands wrapped around her. "Be calm, Catherine."

"Release me right now!"

"I cannot."

She kicked backward and connected with his shin. He grunted, but his hold did not loosen. "Please, *aziz*, do not make this more difficult than it already is."

"You're kidnapping me. I'm not going to make it easy for you!"

"You cannot return to Seattle without me."

"Watch me."

"To do so could very well be to watch you die."

With those startling words, he swung her up into his arms in a hold that immobilized both her legs and arms. He carried her to a waiting helicopter. He lifted her into the helicopter and followed too swiftly for her to jump out again.

"You can't do this." The words were stupid. Patently he could because he was.

With a flick of his hand toward the pilot, the already warming engines revved and then the blades began their rotation. They were in the air within seconds.

There was no hope of conversing over the noise inside the chopper, so she didn't even try.

Trying to talk sense into a madman was difficult enough without having to shout above the sound of the rotor blades.

It was all so unbelievable. Her sheikh, whom she had considered far too civilized for such a thing, was kidnapping her in the best tradition of an Arabian Nights fantasy. Only it wasn't a fantasy. The dark, grim lines of his expression were all too real. So was her anger and the words he'd spoken before bodily carrying her to the helicopter. She might die if she went home without him. What was that all about?

Her thoughts whirled in confusion as the helicopter flew away from the oasis that supported the capital city of Jawhar and toward the region of Kadar.

She looked out the window, straining to see the first glimpse of the mountains bordering Hakim's home.

The helicopter was hovering above an oasis surrounded by tents when Hakim leaned next to Catherine and spoke into her ear so she could hear him. "Put your sweater on."

The desert's evening air was chilly, particularly so far above the ground, so she acquiesced without argument. Besides, even furious with him, her body responded to his nearness in a disastrous way. She didn't want to encourage more of it by arguing and keeping him close to her. She could smell his unique scent, the one her body identified with her lover, her mate and longing that should be as decimated as her heart, but wasn't, went through her.

Using the excuse of pulling her sweater into place, she maneuvered further away from him.

Once the long cardigan was on, he eyed her critically and then leaned forward again until his mouth practically touched her ear. "Can you close the front?"

She shivered as his breath intimately caressed the inside of her ear. He had no right to do this to her. He knew how easily she responded to him. Was he tormenting her on purpose? She shrugged him away with her shoulder.

"It's meant to be worn open." She had raised her voice to a near shout in order to be heard without having to move into his close proximity again. If her traitorous lips got anywhere near his ear, there was no telling what they would do.

The helicopter started to descend.

He said something she couldn't hear. She shook her head to let him know she hadn't gotten it.

He waited to speak again until they were landed and he'd pulled her from the helicopter to stand on the pebbled sand a hundred feet from the oasis and encampment. "It would be better if you could close it. My grandfather is very traditional."

His grandfather? Her attention skittered to the tents within her line of vision. Some were as small as a potting shed and others as large as a cottage with several rooms. They were all cast in a pink glow from the setting sun. One of those dwellings belonged to his grandfather.

"I thought we were going to your palace."

She was in no mood to make nice with more of his family.

"I changed my mind."

"Then change it again. I don't want to meet any more of your relatives."

"That is unfortunate because you are about to."

Who was this man?

He was not the man who had agreed to wait so she could have the wedding of her dreams, nor was he the man who had been so patient with her shyness, who had tempered his passion with gentleness the first time they made love...and every time since.

This man was a stranger.

"I don't know you at all," she whispered.

His body jerked and his eyes narrowed. "I am the man you married."

"But you are not the man I believed you to be. The man I met in Seattle would not have kidnapped me against my will and dropped me in the middle of the desert."

"And yet I am that man. I have been forced to measures I would not have otherwise taken by your irrational behavior."

"That's not true." How dare he say she was not rational?

"Enough of this? You see no perspective but your own. We will talk when you have calmed down."

Judging by the tight reign he had on himself, Hakim had some cooling down to do.

"At least tell me why we're here instead of your palace." They had not planned to come to the Bedouin encampment for another two days.

Her sense of being married to a stranger increased as the shadows cast by the setting sun gave him a hawklike appearance.

He raised his hand and with a flick of his wrist, the helicopter lifted into the air again. His expression was bleak. "There are no phones here."

Her gaze moved from his face to follow the disappearing helicopter. "And no source of transportation?"

But she knew the answer to the question before she asked it. He wasn't taking any chances on her running away.

"Not unless you know how to ride a camel."

She looked away from the sky and back at her husband, expecting dark humor or triumph to be glinting in his eyes after that comment. Neither mood was in evidence in the predator sharp lines of his face.

She licked lips that felt dry. "You know I can't."

"Yes."

"So, in addition to kidnapping me, you intend to make me your prisoner?"

"If that is necessary, yes."

She frowned. "I'd say it is already a fact."

"Only if you choose to see it that way."

"What other way is there to see it?" she asked belligerently.

"You are my wife. You are here to meet my family. It is something we planned days ago. There is nothing sinister in that," said the man who had just sent the only form of escape available to her flying off into the rapidly darkening sky.

"Eventually you will have to take me back to Seattle."

"Yes."

She would have said more, but a shout from behind them silenced her. Hakim raised his hand and called out in Arabic.

"Come, let us go meet my grandfather."

She turned away from him and using the scarf that matched her outfit, she fashioned it like a belt around her waist, pulling one edge of the sweater over the other increasing the modesty of the outfit significantly. "All right."

He surprised her by taking her hand and began leading her toward the largest tent and the delegation that had gathered to meet them. Torches cast light on those assembled. Standing in the center was a man almost as tall as Hakim. The wrinkled leather of his skin and red checked covering on his head worn by sheikhs indicated he could be no other than Hakim's grandfather.

He stepped forward to greet them. "You are welcome among my people." He had spoken in English, clearly for her benefit and she was impressed by the courtesy coming from a man so obviously used to authority.

Hakim stopped a few feet from the other man, released Catherine and then stepped forward to embrace his grandfather. "Father of my mother, I am grateful for your welcome."

He came back to her side, taking her hand in a firm hold once again. "Grandfather, this is my wife, Catherine."

The old man's eyes narrowed. "Your bride, you mean."

Catherine looked to Hakim for an explanation, but he wasn't looking at her. His attention was fixed on his grandfather. A quick dialogue in Arabic commenced. Hakim sounded angry. His grandfather sounded adamant.

It ended with Hakim releasing her hand.

A beautiful woman stepped from behind the man to the old sheikh's right. She wore the traditional dress of a Bedouin woman, the garment black, but embroidered with red, her head and neck covered completely by a black georgette scarf.

She smiled at Catherine. "I am Latifah, wife of Ahmed bin Yusef, sister to Hakim. You are to come with me."

Again Catherine looked at Hakim for understanding.

This time, he was looking at her, his expression grim. "My grandfather does not recognize our marriage because he did not witness it. It has been decreed that you will sleep in my sister's tent tonight. You are no doubt pleased by this turn of events." He inclined his head in acknowledgment of that reality.

"You must go with my sister." His hand reached out as if to touch her, but then dropped back to his side.

"Grandfather has decreed that since I am not yet your husband in the eyes of him and his people, to touch you would dishonor you among them."

The words disconcerted her, but it seemed she had an unwitting ally in the old sheikh.

Still smiling, Latifah touched Catherine's arm. "Come. We have much to do, much to talk about."

CHAPTER TEN

BY LATE afternoon the following day, Catherine thought *much to do* an understatement of monumental proportions.

Evidently a Bedouin wedding was every bit of a production as the one they had already gone through. She wondered when she would see Hakim. She had been cloistered in his sister's tent since her arrival and when Catherine had asked, Latifah had smilingly shrugged. Whenever their grandfather allowed him to visit appeared to be the answer.

She wondered if he arrogantly assumed she was going through with the ceremony, or if he was worried she would follow through on her refusal.

She didn't know her own mind right then. Too much had happened, her emotional wounds too fresh for her to do anything more than try to make it through the day without bursting into tears. Luckily Latifah made it easier, assuming agreement from silence and happiness where there was none.

Throughout the day and while they made preparations for a wedding Catherine was not reconciled to, Latifah talked. She was extremely kind and extremely friendly. She'd told Catherine about growing up in Kadar until she was eight. She had also told Catherine why Hakim had gone to live with King Asad and Latifah had gone to live with her grandfather. Catherine shivered at the memory of what Latifah had told her.

The attempted coup twenty years ago had left their

parents dead. She and Hakim had almost died, too, but the ten-year-old boy had managed to spirit his sister out of the palace under attack and had tracked his grand-father's tribe in the desert. When they had found the Bedouins, both children had been suffering from de-hydration and hunger, but they had been alive.

Catherine thought about a small boy who had lost his parents and taken the responsibility of his younger sis-ter's safety. Her heart ached for him. Because from what Latifah said, Hakim had not only lost his parents, but latter arrangements had effectively severed him from his remaining closest relative.

Latifah had been raised Bedouin and Hakim had been raised to be the Sheikh of Kadar, trusted adopted son to King Asad.

His feelings of obligation toward his king stemmed from more than a simple sense of honor, they stemmed from his emotions as well. How could it be otherwise when the King had become the only consistent entity in Hakim's life?

''And these troublemakers, they are the same ones who threaten the royal family now?'' she asked Latifah.

Latifah's dark brown eyes snapped with anger. ''Yes. Though smaller in number. The sons took over where the fathers left off. It is criminal. They have no popular support and still they attempt these horrendous things. They would have succeeded in their assassination at-tempt on Hakim had he not been so well trained in combat.''

Unwelcome fear jolted through Catherine. ''They tried to kill Hakim?''

''Yes. Did he not tell you? Men. They hide these things and believe they are protecting our feelings.

Women can give birth. Do not tell me we are too weak to know the truth.''

Catherine agreed, but right now she wanted to know more about the assassination attempt, not discuss the misconceptions between the sexes. ''When did this happen?''

''On Hakim's last trip home to Kadar. It upset my grandfather very much and for once he did not complain when Hakim returned to America.''

He'd married her, not only out of duty, she now realized, but out of a very real need to protect his family from the horror of the past. For him, these living visas represented an opportunity to protect his family. Something he could do personally, not just pay for with his great wealth.

She understood that.

She also understood that the concept of barter being exchanged at a marriage was not the same for him as it was for her. That had been brought home as Latifah helped Catherine sew several gold coins onto her headdress for the wedding. It was a dowry provided by the old sheikh in order to show her value to his people.

Among these people, such an exchange was not only acceptable, it was expected.

Her father and King Asad's deal that centered on her marriage to Hakim was in no way out of the ordinary.

In one sense, she could truly comprehend his view of their marriage, but understanding did not lessen the pain. She had believed he loved her and he didn't. She felt betrayed by him, by her father and by her own misreading of the situation. She'd talked herself into believing he loved her, but he'd never used the words. It had all been in her own mind and that made a mockery of the wealth of feeling she had for him.

"What about love?" she asked Latifah as the other woman finished affixing the final coin to the fabric.

Latifah's brows drew together. "What do you mean?"

"Does love have no place in marriage among your people?"

The other woman's eyes widened in shock. "Of course. How can you doubt it? I love my husband very much."

"Does he love you?" Catherine could not help asking.

Latifah's smile was secretive and all woman. "Oh, yes."

"But…"

"Love is very important among our people." Latifah lifted the headdress and admired it.

"Yet your marriages are based on economic gain." Catherine was trying to understand.

Latifah shrugged. "It is expected for love and affection to grow after marriage."

"Does it always?" Did Hakim expect to come to love her? Was he open to the possibility?

Latifah carefully laid the headdress aside and surveyed Catherine. "It is the duty of both husband and wife to give their affection to one another. You must not worry about this. It will come in time."

Catherine met Latifah's exotic eyes with her own. Could a woman so beautiful comprehend her own insecurities? She did not see how. Latifah's husband had probably found it very easy to fall in love with his wife. They shared the same background, the same hopes and expectations and she was stunning to look at.

Hakim, on the other hand, was married to a woman who had been raised very differently from himself. The fact that she was also ordinary and shy only added to the mix of Catherine's insecurities.

That evening, she was allowed to see Hakim under the sharp eyed chaperonage of his grandfather. They had no opportunity to talk about anything of a private nature, which frustrated her. She understood many things about Hakim that had eluded her, but she needed to talk to him before she would commit to going through with the Bedouin marriage.

The fact she was even considering it spoke volumes about the effect his absence from her life for two nights and a day had on her. She missed him and if she missed him this much after such a short absence what would the rest of her life without him be like?

Although the marriage had clearly been a business arrangement, he had made the effort to develop a personal relationship between them. He had shared his time with her, proving to her that they enjoyed one another's company. His friendship was as hard to let go of as his lovemaking.

And that was saying something.

Her body was now permanently addicted to his, the craving he engendered in her a constant pulsing ache in her innermost being. It shamed her she could be so affected by physical need, but when she considered how gloriously he fulfilled those needs, she wanted to weep.

What did she have to look forward to if he let her go? She knew she'd never love another man as she loved Hakim. No matter what he felt for her, the feelings she had for him were too deep, too permanent to ever be repeated with someone else.

When she went to bed that night, it was with a great deal of frustration. The wedding was to take place in two days' time and if those days followed the pattern of this one, she would not get a chance to talk to Hakim.

She lay in the bed of silk quilts and cushions, listening to the sounds of the desert and camp nightlife outside. A group of men walked by and their masculine laughter filtered through the thick wall of the tent. The camels were silent, but not all the animals had gone to sleep.

The air had cooled significantly and she snuggled into the blankets, glad for their layers between her and the cold.

She was on the verge of sleep when a hand closed over her mouth. Adrenaline shot through her system, sending her into fight or flight mode and she jackknifed into a sitting position, only to be trapped in a steel-like grip.

"It is I, Hakim."

As his voice whispered directly into her ear penetrated her terror, she relaxed, her body going almost boneless from relief.

He removed his hand from her mouth.

"What are you doing here?"

"Shh." Again he spoke straight into her ear, his warm breath fanning the always current flicker of desire in her to a small flame. "Do not speak loudly or we will be discovered."

"Okay," she whispered, "but what are you doing here?"

"We must talk."

He helped her to stand and the cold air quickly penetrated her thin nightgown, but he was wrapping her in a cloak that smelled of him before she could voice her discomfort.

He led her outside the tent, via a passageway she had

noticed earlier. It surprised her to discover there was more than one entrance to the outside in the large, but temporary dwelling. Once they were outside, she realized she had forgotten shoes as her tender feet came into contact with sharper objects than sand.

Once again, Hakim seemed to know before she spoke and he swung her up into his arms, carrying her beyond the light cast by the torches of the Bedouin camp.

He stopped and sank gracefully to the ground, keeping her close as he did so. She found herself in her husband's lap and felt the unmistakable evidence of arousal against her hip.

She tried to move away.

He tightened his grip on her. "Relax."

"You're…" She couldn't finish the sentence.

"I know." He sounded disgruntled and angry, but at least she knew his desire for her was real.

She also liked knowing he'd felt the need to talk before the ceremony. It meant he wasn't completely sure of her. His arrogance actually had limits.

She waited for him to talk, but he seemed preoccupied. One hand wrapped in the strands of her hair and his face was averted, as if he was contemplating the stars.

Finally he spoke. "We are to be married by Bedouin ceremony in two days' time."

"So I've been told."

He faced her. "According to Latifah's husband, you have been engaged in preparations all day."

"Yes." If he wanted to know if she planned to go through with it, he could ask.

"Have you considered you might be carrying my child?"

The question was so far from the one she expected

that at first, she did not take it in. When she did, she stopped breathing for several seconds.

Could she be pregnant? With a sinking sensation in the region of her heart, she had to admit it was likely. Their marriage had coincided with the most fertile time in her cycle. It had not been planned that way, but the result could very well be another al Kadar. Her baby. Hakim's baby. *Their* baby.

Her plummeting heart made an unexpected dive for the surface. The thought of carrying Hakim's child was not an unpleasant one, but she could hardly divorce the father of her child before it was even born.

"No."

"No you have not considered it, or no, you are not pregnant?"

"I hadn't considered it."

"That is funny, for I have thought of little else since the first time I planted my seed in your womb."

She went hot all over at his words, becoming even more keenly aware of the hardness under her hip. "You don't know they got planted."

"Considering how frequently we made love, I would say it is very likely."

She couldn't deny it, so she said nothing.

"Is the thought of having my child an unpleasant one?"

She had asked him for truth. She refused to prevaricate herself. "No."

She could feel tension drain from him and only then did she realize how uptight he had really been.

"Will you love my child?"

"How can you ask that?"

"It is not so unreasonable to believe the hatred you hold for the father could be transferred to the child."

"I would never hate my own child." Or any child for that matter. The comment that she hated him, she refused to answer.

"For the sake of our child, will you go through the ceremony in two days' time?"

"We don't know there really is a child." But the thought was a sweet one.

"We do not know there is not."

"It would really shame you if I refused, wouldn't it?" That had become very apparent the more time she spent observing the Bedouin life.

"Yes. It would also cast shame on the child of our union."

He'd latched on to her weakness right away and was obviously intent on making use of it.

"I cannot say vows I don't mean."

"There is no vow of love in the Bedouin ceremony."

He really believed she'd stopped loving him. She wished it was that simple to turn off emotion. It wasn't, but she was not about to share that knowledge with him.

"You married me as part of a business deal."

"I cannot deny this, but that does not negate the reality of the marriage."

She wasn't so sure about that, but she decided to pursue another grievance. "You kidnapped me."

"It was necessary."

"For you to get your way you mean."

"For your safety."

"That doesn't make any sense." How could she be in danger going home to Seattle?

"Threats were made against your life the day after our marriage."

"What? How?"

"A letter to the palace. King Asad showed it to me the day we left."

While she had been making her plans to leave him. No wonder he had had the plane held at the airport.

"It is my duty to protect you. I could not let you go."

"Duty," she said with disgust. She was coming to hate that word.

"Yes, duty. Responsibility. I learned these words very young. I am a sheikh. I cannot dismiss my promises as easily as you do your wedding vows."

That infuriated her and she jumped off his lap to land on her bottom in the cooling desert sand. She scrambled to her feet. "I'm not dismissing them."

He stood, too, casting a dark and ominous shadow in the moonlight. "Are you not? You threaten divorce hours after promising me a lifetime."

Okay, maybe from his perspective she was dismissing those vows, but they didn't count. "I was tricked into them."

"You were wooed."

"How can you say that?"

"It is the truth."

His truth.

She sighed. "I should get back before your sister realizes I've left the tent."

"We are not done talking."

"You mean I haven't agreed to your plans."

"I want your promise you will go through with the ceremony."

"I want some time to think."

"You have two days to think."

"What will you do if I say *no*?"

Instead of answering, he kissed her. Anger pulsated

in that kiss, a fury she had not even realized he was holding in, but there was passion too. Desire. And seduction. When he pulled back, she was limp in his arms and barely standing. "You will go through the ceremony so that you are my wife in my grandfather's eyes. Then I will make love to you and you will forget this talk of divorce."

His complacent belief that he could seduce her utterly to his will made her angry. So she lashed out. "Why not? We've already been through one sham wedding. Why not another?"

She fully expected him to explode, but he didn't. Tension filled his body, but he merely said, "Indeed."

He scooped her up into his arms and then carried her back to the tent, not putting her down again until he reached her bed. He leaned over and spoke with his lips so close, their breath mingled. "Good night, *aziz*."

Then he kissed her. She expected another passionate assault on her senses. More anger. More seduction. She got a gentle caress that left her lips tingling.

Then he was gone.

Catherine wrinkled her nose, both from the sight and the smell of the camel kneeling on all four legs before her.

Latifah had informed Catherine that her husband had ridden this animal to victory in the past three camel races. The knowledge was small comfort as she climbed into the boxlike chair on the camel's back. She'd never even ridden a horse and here she was, getting ready to ride a camel.

She adjusted herself on her seat, gasping as the box swayed with her movements. It was tall enough for her to sit fully erect, but she had to curl her legs under her because there was no place else to put them.

She was supposed to ride in this rather daunting conveyance to her wedding. Evidently this was the Bedouin equivalent to the romantic horse and carriage she'd dreamed of and been forced to discard as impractical in the rainy winter weather of Seattle.

The old sheikh led the camel himself, saying that since her father was not there to do it, he would be pleased at the honor.

She felt as if a thousand eyes were on her as the camel made its sedate pace toward where the ceremony was to be held.

Catherine kept her head down, but peeked through her lashes at the desert people who had gathered to watch her and Hakim marry according to their tradition. Small silver bells on the ornate necklace she wore made a tinkling sound as her body moved with the jarring gait of the camel.

When they reached the site for the marriage, the old sheikh helped Catherine down from the camel and led her to take her place beside Hakim. She didn't look at him during the ceremony, but kept her gaze focused downward as Latifah had instructed.

The ceremony itself didn't take very long, but the Mensaf, a dinner prepared to celebrate their union, did. The men and women ate separately and came together only afterward for the entertainment. They sat in the open air with fires going around them. The wood was so dry, hardly any smoke emitted from the fires, but the scent of burning chicory filled the air. Men played instruments and women sang, their voices beautiful in their Eastern harmony.

Hakim interpreted the words for her, his voice husky in her ear, his fingers curled around her wrist.

She could not ignore the way his touch affected her and the growing desires in her body, not after four nights away from their marriage bed. By the time Latifah led Catherine to Hakim's quarters in his grandfather's tent, it was quite late and she was jittery with pent-up feelings.

Lit with hanging lanterns, the room was surprisingly large. Richly colored silks covered the interior walls of the tent and the floor was made of the beautifully woven rugs the Bedouin women had become famous for. Hakim's bed was in the center of the room.

It was too elaborate to be called a pallet even though the large cushion for sleeping reposed on the floor with no frame under it. A multitude of pillows indicated the head of the bed. They were framed by billowing white silk that draped from a round frame hanging from the tent's ceiling.

It was like a tent within a tent.

Other than the impressive bed, there were few other items in the spacious room. Big Turkish pillows, obviously for sitting, were arranged around a small table.

She opted to sit on one of the pillows rather than the bed to wait for Hakim. Unfamiliar with the customs of his grandfather's people, she had no idea how long her husband would be. She could hear the revelry continuing in the camp and then she heard the unmistakable tenor of her husband's rich voice just outside the wall of the tent.

As her attention fixed on the doorway through which he would come, it struck her how like her fantasy her current predicament was.

She'd been kidnapped by a sheikh and waited for him

to have his way with her, but unlike the daydreams, Hakim was flesh and blood. She could touch him and he would touch her.

She shivered in anticipation at the thought.

Hakim paused outside the entrance to his chamber.

Catherine waited inside. She'd charmed Latifah with her sweetness, impressed his grandfather with her humility and scandalized the women who had helped Latifah prepare Catherine for the wedding by refusing to have her hair hennaed.

However, she had been very quiet throughout the evening's festivities. At least she had not refused to go through with the wedding. He had not been sure until he saw his grandfather leading the camel that she would actually go through with it, but then she considered it a sham. *Another* sham.

He would show her tonight there was nothing fake about their marriage.

He brushed aside the covering over the opening into the room and went inside.

The sight of her sitting on a pillow on the far side of the room stopped him. She had removed her headdress and it rested in her lap. Her hair hung loose, its dark honey strands glistening with sweet smelling oil. He inhaled the fragrance, taking in her distinctly feminine scent as he did so.

"My grandfather is pleased with you."

Her eyes flickered, their blue depths turbulent with emotion. "Does he know why you married me?"

"He does not know of my uncle's arrangement with your father, no."

She lifted the gold laden scarf. "Latifah told me this

is considered quite a dowry for a bride, even the bride of a sheikh.''

Hakim wished he knew what she was thinking. ''Grandfather values you.''

She looked down, her hair falling to shield her face from his gaze. Her small, feminine fingers traced the patterns on the coins for several seconds of silence.

Her hand stilled and her head came up. ''Do you?''

''Do I value you?''

''Yes.''

''Can you doubt it?'' She was his wife. Someday, God willing, she would finally understand what that meant to a man raised as he had been raised.

''If I didn't doubt it, I wouldn't be asking.''

The reminder of her mistrust angered him, but he forced himself to speak in a mild tone, without recriminations. ''On the day we arrived in Jawhar, I made you a promise.''

She frowned, her lovely skin puckering between her brows. ''You promised never to lie to me again.''

''And I have not.''

She nodded, apparently accepting that at last.

''I made a promise before that, little kitten.''

Her face showed her confusion. It was a mark of how impacted she had been by later revelations that she had forgotten something that had been very important to her at the time.

''I promised to always put your needs and desires first from this time forward. Tell me how I could value you more?''

''Are you saying that if it came between something your family wanted and what I wanted, you would choose my wants over theirs?'' Her voice was laden with skepticism.

"Yes. That is what I am saying."

"So, if I said I didn't want you to sponsor their living visas?"

"Could you say that and mean it if their lives were in danger?" he asked instead of answering her question.

Her head dropped, her face hidden from him again. "No."

Her continued refusal to see the good in their marriage and in him, frustrated him. "You are very pessimistic."

She jolted, her head coming up. "What?"

"You see only the negative."

CHAPTER ELEVEN

CATHERINE felt Hakim's words like an arrow piercing her. "I don't see only the negative." But even as she said the words, she wondered at their truth.

His expression told her he didn't have to wonder. He knew she was lying. "You would dismiss our marriage as nothing because of an agreement that has no bearing on our lives together. You seek new evidence at every turn to justify your mistrust of me and your cheapening of our marriage."

"I did not cheapen our marriage!" How dare he say that? She had loved him. It was his and her father's deceit that had cheapened the marriage and she said so.

"I did not dismiss you as nothing and demand divorce the day after we were wed. I did not refuse you the comfort of my body or the affection of my heart. You are angry because *love*," he said the word scathingly, "did not motivate my proposal of marriage. Yet you professed your *love* for me and then rejected me and threatened to dishonor me before my people. What is this love?"

Each charge affected her conscience like a prosecuting attorney's court indictment. He had never said he loved her and yet he had treated her with consideration. She had said she loved him, but then threatened divorce within thirty-six hours of their marriage.

"I..." She didn't know what to say.

His words were true and yet it had not been a weakness in her love that had made her do those things, but

146

the strength of her pain. Of her sense of rejection, but he had never actually rejected her.

"You are no doubt sitting there right now planning to tell me not to touch you. No matter that you are my wife. You do not care if I ache with wanting for you. No doubt you will rejoice in the knowledge I am suffering."

"No, I—"

He rode right over her words. "You can easily spurn the intimacy between us."

"It's not easy," she cried.

He snorted, clearly unimpressed with her response. "I have promised you honesty, do I not deserve the same?"

"I'm not lying."

"Are you saying you plan to share my bed?"

"Yes." She had already decided that for the sake of her pride, she would not fight him on this. She would rather walk back into intimacy with Hakim under her own steam than deny him and be seduced into his bed anyway. She loved and wanted him too much to deny him.

That fast, his eyes heated with a desire that burned her. He started walking toward her, but she put out her hand.

"Wait."

He stopped.

Before another storm of anger could rise between them, she quickly held up the headdress still clutched in her other hand. "I need to give you this."

His brows drew together in puzzlement, his eyes glittered with wariness. "Why?"

She took a deep breath and then let it out slowly, gathering her thoughts and courage at the same time. "In essence, you bought me with a mining permit."

She had taken a bit to work this all out in her head, but though her father had suggested the marriage, she felt as if she had been bartered in a business deal. She needed to redress that before she could share her body with Hakim again.

When he would have protested, she waved him silent.

"When you accept this gold," she said, indicating the heavily weighted headdress, "I am buying you. It makes us even."

She prayed he would understand and not make fun of her or remind her that his own grandfather had provided the dowry.

He did neither. He looked at the gold and then back at her face. "This is important to you? That we are even?"

"Yes."

"And when I accept your dowry, it is so?"

She nodded.

His eyes darkened with comprehension and he put his hand out to receive the gold. "May you find as much contentment with the exchange as I have done."

He meant as he had done before she found out the truth, but she didn't correct him. She wanted this night to be free of the weight of her father's bartered deal or even Hakim's cultural expectations of such a marriage. She wanted to make love on a level playing field.

She released the headdress into his hands.

Then she untied the gold belt around her hips, letting it fall to the woven rug beneath her feet.

Hakim went completely still, his black eyes fixed on her with almost frightening intensity.

She took advantage of his stillness to remove her dress and the garment under it, letting both glide down her body to pool around her feet. She wasn't wearing a bra and the way his gaze locked onto her naked torso told her he appreciated that fact.

Her nipples, which had already peaked in anticipation of her husband's touch, puckered into firmer rigidity under the heat of his look, stinging with the need to have his mouth on them. Her unfettered breasts swelled, making her skin feel tight and sensitive while other intimate tissues became inflamed, pulses of anticipatory pleasure vibrating trough them.

She walked toward him, the tiny silver bells on her necklace and anklets jingling with each step, her breasts swaying in a way that should have made her blush. For the first time, it didn't. It only increased her sense of feminine power because his eyes locked onto that swaying movement and he began to breathe faster.

When she reached her husband, she pushed his *abaya* off his shoulders. "Let me undress you."

He allowed her to remove his head covering and *egal*.

She let her fingers run through his thick, but short curling hair, reveling in the silky feel against her skin. Reveling also in her right to touch him in this way, to see him as no other woman in Jawhar had the right to see him.

He helped her remove his white tunic, the muscles of his chest rippling as he stretched to take it off.

The flat brown disks of his male nipples drew her attention and her desire. She brushed her fingers over them, feeling her own pleasure as they responded immediately to her touch.

"Yes. Touch me. Show me you desire me as I desire you."

His words sent excitement arcing through her and a determination to do as he said, to show her desire. She leaned forward and licked each nipple, then swirled her tongue around them, tasting the saltiness of his skin, smelling the masculine scent of his body.

His hands clamped on either side of her head. "The sultry air of the desert has turned you into a temptress."

She smiled and took the small, hard nipple into her mouth, sucking on it until he crushed her body to his with an agonized groan. She wiggled against him until her fingers could reach the drawstring on his loose fitting white pants. She tugged at it and it came undone so that the only thing holding them up was the way her body was pressed so tightly against his.

Tilting her head back, her eyes met his. "Take them off."

"You think because you have bought me, you can order me like a slave?" The warm humor in his eyes told her he was joking and not offended.

She gave him her best haughty look. "Of course."

His brows rose, but then they lowered and his look became predatory. "Then you are my slave also."

She found herself swallowing nervously. The game was taking a turn she hadn't expected. "Yes."

He said nothing, but he let her go to step back and push his pants down his thighs. Sleek satin hardness sprang up to greet her.

Remembering the pleasure she felt when he was inside her was exciting her.

"Take off your last covering." The way he said it sent shivers of desire and trepidation down her limbs.

All of a sudden it felt as if the small bit of lace was indeed her last covering, or protection, against him.

But she didn't need protection against him. Not now. She wanted what was about to happen. Very much.

She pushed the scrap of fabric down her thighs, exposing damp blonde curls.

"Come to me."

She took the step forward that separated them, stopping so close to him that the tip of his manhood brushed the soft skin of her stomach.

He reached down, grabbed her hand and led it to the rigid shaft between them. "Touch me."

She allowed her trembling fingers to curl around him. The hardness encased in warm satin fascinated her and she stroked him to the base. He made an incoherent sound of need and his head tipped back, his hands clenched at his sides.

She reversed her stroking and allowed her thumb to flick over the end of him.

His entire body racked in a giant shudder. *"More."* Both demand and plea, she found it impossible to deny him.

She did not want to deny him.

Touching him with gentle then firm strokes, she gave him more...and more...and more.

His entire body had drawn taut when he grabbed her wrist to still her hand. "Enough."

He took several deep breaths, his body shuddering. "Now it is your turn."

For him to touch her?

"To command," he clarified and she smiled.

They were still playing their game.

She didn't think she had the temerity to tell him to touch her. "Carry me to bed." It was where she wanted to be.

He didn't hesitate. He lifted her in strong arms and carried her to the bed in the center of the room. He knelt on the coverlet with her still in his arms and then released her legs so they knelt facing each other, his arms locked around her waist. He lowered his head and kissed her.

The kiss seared her lips with heat and touched something deep inside of her.

He was her husband and she wanted him, would always want him.

His lips broke away from hers to trail down her neck.

"I need you, Hakim."

His head came up, ebony eyes blazing into her own. "I have ached for you."

"You have me."

Triumph flared in his features. "Yes. I have you. I will never let you go."

She didn't want to think about the future. She wanted to concentrate on the present. She pulled his head down and kissed him, opening her mouth in invitation against his lips. The warmth of his tongue invaded her and soon the kiss was devouring and carnal.

Their game forgotten, Hakim made love to her with his hands, his mouth and ultimately, his body. When he exploded inside of her, she almost fainted as her own orgasm joined his.

Afterward, they lay entwined, their bodies sweat soaked.

He disengaged himself from her clinging arms and she moaned in protest, too wasted to actually form words with her mouth.

"Shh, little kitten. I want only to make you comfortable."

Soon, she found herself tucked under a silk quilt, surrounded by Hakim and pillows. He had extinguished the lights and released the chord on the bed hangings so it fell in a circular tent around them, an extra layer of privacy.

She snuggled into his side.

"Little kitten suits you well. You cuddle like a small cat, content to warm yourself with my flesh."

"You make me feel small."

"It is only in your mind that you are some Amazon creature."

She kissed the warm brown skin of his chest. "I know, but I like how you make me feel just the same." Because he didn't just make her feel small. He made her feel cherished.

"I am pleased this is so."

Playing idly with the black curling hair on his chest, she asked, "How long are we staying here?"

"We can go to our home in Kadar as soon as you like."

"Will it offend your grandfather if we do not stay longer?" Their short stay in King Asim's palace had been planned as part of their journey, but they had originally discussed staying among his grandfather's people for a few days.

"He would prefer we stayed long enough for me to race his favorite camel."

"When are the races?"

"In two days' time. Two other encampments will participate."

"I don't mind staying if you don't." She liked his sister and found the Bedouin way of life fascinating.

He hugged her to him in blatant approval. "It would please me to stay."

"Will you teach me to ride a camel?"

"Are you sure you want to learn? You looked very nervous today as you rode in the bride's coach."

"The box swayed. I thought it might fall off."

"I would never allow you to be at such risk."

For the first time, it struck her that this stranger he'd become was no stranger at all. He was Hakim. A complex man with many facets to himself. At once hard and unbending and then tender and protective, but always at the core the man she had fallen in love with, her sheikh.

Catherine enjoyed the next two days very much.

Latifah was a wonderful companion and she laughingly taught Catherine the rudimentary moves of Eastern dance while Hakim spent time with his grandfather. The second lesson was a little more difficult than the first as it came after Catherine's first lesson riding a camel. She was sore from the exercise, but the dance limbered up her muscles and Hakim's sensual massage that night completed her recuperation.

Dancing and camel riding weren't the only things she was learning while staying in the encampment. Hakim took great pains to teach her the extent of pleasure her body was capable of experiencing each night. When they were making love, she found it easy to forget the real reasons for their marriage.

As she watched her husband and Ahmed vie for first place in the camel race, ulterior motives for her marriage were the furthest thing from her mind. She was too terrified to think of anything else.

"I didn't know camels could move that fast."

Latifah laughed. "They are magnificent, are they not?"

"But what if the camel stumbles? What if Hakim is thrown?"

More laughter met her questions. "Hakim?" Latifah asked with clear disbelief.

"He's a man like any other, made of flesh and blood, bones that can break." Okay, maybe he wasn't like any other man, but he was still breakable.

Latifah became serious. "You care very much for my brother, do you not?"

"Yes," Catherine admitted, without tearing her gaze from the racing camels. "I love him. It's why I married him."

"I am glad. He deserves this love, I think."

Catherine sucked in a terrified breath as Hakim made a move with his camel that looked incredibly risky.

"He is an excellent rider," Latifah tried to reassure her. "He often wins the race, much to my husband's chagrin. It is good for Ahmed not to win every time."

It was Catherine's turn to laugh at Latifah's complacent statement.

Latifah laughed with her. "I am not disloyal, but my husband has been known to be insufferable after winning a race."

"Arrogance runs in the family, does it?" She'd learned that Ahmed and Hakim were cousins.

The other woman's eyes twinkled. "Yes."

"So, you're wishing the insufferable winner syndrome on me instead?"

"I believe my brother already considers himself the winner. He is well pleased with you for his wife."

Two hours later, Catherine and the winner of the camel races boarded another black helicopter. Again, there was little opportunity for communication as the helicopter flew through the sky, but unlike before, Hakim took Catherine's hand firmly in his, keeping it captive for the entire flight.

Her first view of Hakim's palace was an aerial one. Nowhere near as huge as the Palace of Jawhar, it was nevertheless an impressive structure. Domed roofs and tinted sandstone gave the hilltop structure a distinctively Middle Eastern look.

The helicopter landed in a flat valley several hundred feet from the palace. Men wearing the distinct black of King Asad's private guard were there to meet them along with an SUV to drive them and their luggage to the palace.

Hakim insisted on giving her a tour of the palace right off. She was right that it wasn't nearly as big as his uncle's palace, but she was still overwhelmed by the time he led her up a winding staircase. It seemed to go on forever before it ended at the entrance to a glass domed room.

It was an observatory, obviously built many years ago. Books on stargazing lined one wall. Some were in English, some French and some Arabic.

However, the books could not hold her attention long, not when in the center of the room sat a table and on that table resided a vintage George Lee and Sons telescope in perfect condition. She walked toward it as if drawn by a force greater than herself, her hand outstretched to touch.

Her fingertips brushed along the barrel. "It's beautiful."

"I believed you would like it."

She spun around to face him. "I thought, you know, that you faked your interest in ancient stargazing so we'd have something in common."

His mouth twisted in a grimace. "The telescope was my father's as was the passion for this hobby, but I soon found myself interested beyond pursuing it merely as a means to get to know you."

Why they met was taking on less and less significance the longer she stayed with him. She was sure that had been his plan when he kidnapped her. "Will you continue to attend meetings for the Antique Telescope Society with me?"

"I would enjoy the opportunity to do so."

She smiled.

"I meant to present the telescope to you as a gift before our wedding in the desert. It would have pleased my father for a true devotee of his favorite hobby to have it, particularly his daughter by marriage."

"I don't know what to say."

He took her hands in his, his eyes compelling her agreement. "Say you will accept it."

She sensed that in accepting it, she was tacitly accepting the permanence of that marriage. Was she ready to do that?

No matter what he felt for her, ultimately, it came down to life with Hakim and life without him. The possibility that she might carry his child weighed heavily against life without him. It was much too soon to tell, but she could not shake the feeling she was pregnant.

But even without a baby, the last few days had shown her the richness of life with him. Did she really want to return to the colorless life she had without him in it?

"You've fought very hard to keep this marriage," she said.

"I will never let you go."

"I have a say in it, Hakim."

He spun around and pounded one fist into the other palm. "When will you cease to fight me on this? You are my wife," he raged, shocking her into stillness with his unexpected anger. "I will not let you go. You are the mother of my children. Even now, you could carry my baby. Do you consider this when you make your plans to leave me?"

"I haven't *made* any plans." At least not since the first attempt to leave Jawhar on her own.

She laid her hand over her belly, a warm feeling suffusing her, even in the face of her husband's anger. "Do you think I might truly be pregnant?"

He spun around to face her. "If not, it is not for lack of trying on my part."

The admission stunned her. "You'd do anything to keep our marriage."

"Believe it."

He'd promised her fidelity, honesty and that she would come first in his consideration. It was a better recipe for marriage than many she'd seen and according to Latifah, love came later. Even so, there was no guarantee he would ever come to love her.

And if he had loved her, what was the guarantee he would always do so? In Hakim she had a husband who would always keep his promises.

"I don't want to end our marriage. I don't want to leave you."

His smile sent her pulses racing. In that moment of her capitulation, he looked marvelously happy. He could not be so happy if she personally meant nothing to him.

She put her hand out. ''Let's get a little more practice in at starting a family.''

Rich, deep laughter reverberated around her as Hakim led her to their room and a night of loving unlike any they had yet shared.

CHAPTER TWELVE

A LITTLE over three weeks later, they flew back into Sea-Tac, greeted by the typical gray skies and wet weather of a Seattle winter. Catherine mourned the loss of the warm sunshine of Hakim's desert home. Her husband clearly reveled in his Kadar lifestyle. Being honest with herself, she had to admit she had as well.

A great deal of it had been Hakim. He'd been so attentive and wanted to share every aspect of his life as a sheikh with her. She'd visited the settlements in his region, learned the only library available was at the palace and discovered an instant rapport with the people they came into contact with.

She had enjoyed their warmth and unreserved welcome for their sheikh's wife. The only downside had been the many requests the people made for Hakim's return. His political responsibilities were being seen to by a cousin from his father's side of the family, but his people wanted the Sheikh of Kadar to come home permanently.

She didn't understand his refusal to even discuss it. Could King Asad truly be cruel enough to expect Hakim to give up his homeland to oversee business interests? It didn't fit with the man she'd observed on their second visit to the capital.

Hakim drove them home from the airport in his Jaguar.

"We will have to arrange a visit with your parents now that we are back in Washington."

She noticed he never called Seattle home.

She swallowed a sigh. She'd have to face her father sometime. "Does Mom know? About Dad's deal with your uncle I mean."

Hakim's jaw clenched and he shook his head once in negation. "He did not think she would understand."

Just as Catherine had not *understood*, but she was glad her mom had not known. It would hurt that much more to think both her parents had been so willing to barter her life away.

"I'll call Mom and schedule something in a couple of weeks."

"Your father is scheduled to travel to Kadar the week after next to investigate the most likely mining sites."

He certainly wasn't letting any grass grow under his feet. "I guess we'll have to wait to see him until after he gets back."

With a little luck, it would take him several weeks to choose a site. By then she might have her emotions under control enough to see him without going totally ballistic.

"Why not before he goes? Surely this can be arranged."

She sighed. "I'm not sure I want it arranged."

"I thought you had reconciled yourself to our marriage."

Her gaze snapped to him. His jaw was taut, his expression unreadable.

"I am."

"Then why do you not want to see your father?"

"Because he betrayed me."

"As you believed I betrayed you."

She couldn't deny it. "Yes." She hated this. Everything had been fine until he brought up her father.

"And you cannot forgive."

That stopped her. She'd forgiven Hakim because forgiveness had been necessary to the healing of the wound in their marriage. But she'd never told him, assuming he knew because she'd stayed with him.

Apparently he didn't.

"I do forgive you."

"And your father? He wants only what is best for you."

"He made my marriage into a business deal."

"I have only met him a few times, but this seems to be his way. To do what he knows. To believe he knows best."

It was an accurate summation of her father's take-no-prisoners approach to business and life. And no doubt about it, he understood business better than people.

"Catherine?"

What could she say? She could not regret having Hakim in her life. Her heart had been shredded by the men's deceit, but it had not ended with the pain and the past few weeks had given her hope that perhaps one day her marriage would truly be one of love, not a business deal. "I'll call Mom and get something scheduled. I want to see Felicity too."

"You and your sister are very close."

"She's always been there for me."

"This is a good thing. Latifah is very important to me, but after the attempted coup we were no longer raised in the same household. We are not close."

It always surprised her when he opened up with something like this. He kept his deeper emotions under guard so much of the time, except in bed. Then his passion was as volatile as a live volcano.

LUCY MONROE   163

"What about your cousins?" He'd been raised with them. Had they taken the role of brothers?

"It was determined early on that I would accept the role of diplomat and so I was educated abroad from the age of twelve."

"It must have been lonely growing up being part of a family, but having a destiny that placed you on the outside in many ways."

He shrugged, his powerful shoulders shifting with the movement. "I am no longer alone. With you, I am very much on the inside."

The sexual innuendo made her blush, but at the same time, her eyes filled with unaccountable tears. She'd been extremely emotional the past week and couldn't help wondering if the fact her menses were two weeks late had something to do with it. Had all Hakim's concentrated efforts paid off?

She blinked away the moisture and went for an expression of amusement. "I'll say." She gave him her best version of a lascivious wink and squeezed his thigh.

Deep, masculine laughter erupted around her as he caught her hand in his. "Behave, wife."

"I thought I was behaving, *husband*." She drew the word out in a long, slow, intimate breath of sound.

His fingers laced with hers. "We are fully reconciled, are we not?"

"Yes."

He was silent for a couple of miles. "You are no longer considering divorce?"

She was surprised he felt the need to ask. "No. I told you I was committed to our marriage."

"And you do not think I am lower than the underside of a lizard in the desert?"

That shocked a giggle from her. "No. I don't think that."

"Then why have you not repeated your avowal of love since the day after our wedding?"

Tension seeped into her body, making her muscles contract. "You didn't marry me for love."

"Does this negate your love for me?"

What difference could it possibly make to him?

She pulled her hand from Hakim's and turned to look out the window. Gray sky and wet concrete made an uninspiring view. "What do you want me to say?"

"I want you to tell me you love me."

The blatant request buffeted nerves that she thought had settled. She could make her own demand for the same thing and did not doubt he would comply. It was his duty to come to love her, so he would will himself to do so, but she didn't want a duty vow. She wanted the same hot cauldron of emotions that seethed inside her to churn in him.

When she didn't answer he brushed her cheek. "Is it so hard, little kitten?"

"I'm not sure this is the best place for this discussion."

She could see him return his hand to the steering wheel out of the corner of her eye. His jaw clenched for the second time in twenty minutes. "Perhaps you are right."

She hated feeling like all the rapport they had shared for the past few weeks was going up in smoke.

How could she explain that telling him she loved him made her feel vulnerable? That somehow keeping the words locked inside protected her heart from his indifference.

Only he *wasn't* indifferent.

He wanted to hear her words of love. Could it be that he was coming to love her? Did he feel just as vulnerable as she did because she hadn't told him she loved him since learning of the real reasons behind their marriage? Perhaps by trying to protect her own feelings, she was not leaving room for him to express his, or at least to allow his to grow into something stronger than dutiful affection.

She turned to look at his tense profile. "I do love you." Her voice was low, almost a whisper, but he heard her.

His grip on the steering wheel tightened until his knuckles showed white. "You are right. This is not the place for such declarations."

Hurt by the apparent rejection of her words, she demanded, "Why?"

"Because I now want to make love to you with painful fervor and it will be at least fifteen minutes before we reach our home."

Catherine called her father's office the next day. They needed to talk. But he had flown to South America on business and wasn't expected back for several days. Catherine made an appointment to see him before he left the country again, this time to the Kadar Province in Jawhar.

The day before her appointment with her father, Catherine was in the living room of her and Hakim's penthouse, curled up on the sofa, a book on ancient astronomy in her lap. She traced a picture of a telescope very similar to the one Hakim had given her after their wedding and remembered their days in Kadar.

Hakim had spent the first ten years of his childhood

in that palace. She could imagine him as a small boy, learning to ride a camel, teasing his little sister as boys do, climbing into his mother's lap for a cuddle when he was tired.

Catherine gently touched her stomach and pictured the same things with her own child. Only she was having a really hard time picturing them here in Seattle. The palace in Kadar had felt like a home, a grand one, but a home nonetheless. Their penthouse felt like a yuppie launching pad. It wasn't just the difference between Hakim's penthouse apartment and the palace in Kadar, either.

It was more. It was millennia of tradition, family and political responsibilities, an entirely different way of life to the one her child would know here.

A way of life she thought she could embrace. A way of life she knew her husband missed.

"Hello, little kitten. Did you have a good day at the library?"

She'd been so lost in her thoughts, she hadn't heard him come in.

She looked up and smiled. "Hi. It's been a wonderful day. Come and sit by me and I'll tell you all about it."

He shrugged off his suit jacket and loosened his tie before tugging it off. By the time he joined her on the couch, the top two buttons on his dress shirt were undone. Dark hair peeked out of the opening.

She reached out and brushed a fingertip along the open V. "You're a sinfully sexy man, Hakim."

Ebony eyes burned with instant desire. "It pleases me you find it so."

Her own eyes fluttered shut as he lowered his head to kiss her, his customary greeting when they'd been apart for longer than a few minutes. There was something desperate in his lips she didn't understand and she automatically sought to sooth with her response, surrendering completely to his touch.

Ten minutes later, she was lying across his lap, the small pearl buttons on her sweater undone along with the front clasp on her bra. His hand gently cupped her breast, one thumb brushing over an already hardened nipple.

"To come home to such a greeting makes up for a lot." His words whispered against her neck between small, biting kisses.

"And what am I making up for, the lousy traffic in downtown Seattle?" she asked, breathless with rapidly spiraling desire.

He husked a laugh and hugged her tightly to him.

She leaned back a little, wanting to see his eyes. "I've got news."

His brows rose. "Do not hesitate to tell me."

Her lips tilted in a smile. She loved it when he talked all sheikhlike. "As of Monday, I'll be part-time at the library and I've explained that if you need to travel for business I am going with you."

She wasn't sure how black eyes could darken, but his did...with pleasure. "I like this news very much."

"I thought you would." She also hoped he would feel free to make more trips to Jawhar if he knew she could go with him on short notice.

She snuggled more firmly into his lap, reveling in the feel of his hardened flesh under her bottom. "There's more."

He groaned and the hand on her breast contracted. "Perhaps it can wait."

She wiggled again for good measure, but shook her head. "I want to tell you now."

His hands locked on her hips to stop their movement. "Then tell me before I ravish you here on the sofa."

"There's a reason I wanted to go part-time."

His head had fallen back and his eyes were closed, his nostrils dilated with arousal. "What is that?"

"All your effort paid off."

His eyes flew open and he looked at her with reproach. "I did not demand you cut your hours at work."

"I didn't go part-time because you wanted me to," she assured him.

The twist of his lips said her answer had not reassured.

"I altered my work schedule to accommodate an upcoming change in our family." She leaned forward and kissed his lips very softly, then with their mouths only separated by a breath, she said, "I'm going to have your baby."

If she had not known better, she would have thought a spasm of pain crossed his face, but it was gone in a flash to be replaced by unadulterated joy.

"Thank you," he whispered against her lips and then he kissed her.

It was the most tender expression of affection he had ever shown her. Then he broke into speech in Arabic, his hand moving to cover her belly, his mouth kissing her all over her face, neck and chest.

He cupped her breast. "My baby will suckle here," he said with awe.

Tears filled her eyes. "Yes."

He pressed a gentle kiss to one rigid peak and then the other. He moved until he had her laid out on the couch before him; somewhere along the way, their clothes had disappeared. He paid homage to her breasts again, then moved his mouth to press a ring of kisses around her navel. "My child is nourished and protected here in the warmth of your body."

Her fingers tangled in the thick black hair on his head and tears of love, joy, and pleasure swam in her eyes.

His mouth rested over the blond curls at the apex of her thighs. When his tongue darted out to part the folds of her femininity and seek her pleasure spot, she arched up off the couch. "Hakim!"

He pressed her thighs apart and continued to make love to her with his mouth until she was shuddering in exquisite release. He moved up her body, taking possession of her with one sure thrust. "From this pleasure we made life between us."

"Oh, darling…Hakim. My love."

His lips cut off any more endearments, but her heart continued to utter them, beating out a rhythm of her love that he had to have felt.

He established a pace that soon had her arching in renewed tension, but this time when she went soaring among the stars, he was with her.

Afterward he collapsed on top of her and she brushed her hands down his back, petting him, loving him. "I love you."

His head came up and his face wore the most serious expression she had ever seen. "Do not stop loving me, I beg of you."

"Never," she promised fiercely. "I will always love you."

The warmth of his desert home was in his smile. "Then all is worth it, jewel of my heart. For the gift of your love, the gift of our child makes every sacrifice of no consequence."

"What sacrifice?"

But he was kissing her again and any thought of conversation melted under the fire of his physical love.

Catherine dressed for success for her meeting with Harold Benning. Her straight black skirt, short-sleeved black sweater and hip-length hound's-tooth jacket gave her badly needed confidence. She hadn't had a heart-to-heart talk with her parents since before puberty.

He looked up from his desk, a telephone pressed to his ear, when she walked in. Wariness chased shock across his features.

He said something into the phone and then hung it up. "Catherine."

Now that she was here, Catherine didn't know where to start.

"Would you like a cup of coffee, something to drink?"

She shook her head. "Not really. I want to talk to you."

"About your marriage." It was a statement, not a question.

"How did you know?"

Her dad leaned back in his leather executive chair, his pose relaxed, but his expression watchful. "Hakim called from Jawhar to tell me you knew about the mining deal."

Her hands clenched at her sides. "It isn't exactly your average mining deal, though is it? Instead of paying for the privilege to mine in Jawhar, you bartered your daughter like some medieval tyrant."

Her dad's brown eyes snapped with reproach. "It wasn't like that."

She sat down in one of the chairs in front of his desk and crossed her legs, trying to project an air of casualness she did not feel. "Why don't you tell me what it was like?"

"You know your mother and I have been worried about your lack of a social life for years. When this business with King Asad came up, I saw a way to kill two birds with one stone is all. I didn't do a damn thing to hurt you."

She shot to her feet and leaned across his desk until their faces were inches apart. "You didn't do anything to hurt me? Just how do you think I felt when I discovered the man I loved didn't love me, that he married me as part of a business deal? Let me tell you. It hurt! It hurt a lot."

Her dad sank back into his chair like a puppet whose strings had been cut, but he didn't say anything.

She didn't need him to.

She was in full throttle now. "Let me tell you about hurting. I found out that both my husband and my father had lied to me. I knew I wasn't as important to you as Felicity, but I never thought you saw me as an expendable possession!"

He flinched and passed his hands across his face. "You aren't expendable to me. I didn't sell you into slavery in a third-world country, Catherine. I fixed you up with a business associate."

"Without telling me."

His expression turned belligerent at that. "Hell no, I didn't tell you. You would have run a mile in the opposite direction."

"So you told Hakim how to manage an *accidental* meeting."

He shrugged. "It seemed the best way to get you to give him a chance. Listen to me, Catherine. The laser treatment got rid of the scars on your face, but that wasn't enough. Your mom and I thought once the scars were gone, everything would be okay, you'd date like your sister, get married one day. Have a life.''

She looked away, not wanting to see the years-old pity burning in his eyes.

''It didn't work that way, though. You don't trust people, especially men. Hell, maybe that's my fault. I ignored you because I couldn't fix your problem. And you felt rejected because of it. I was wrong, but I can't change it now. Maybe you were afraid of being rejected again. I don't know, but until Hakim, you kept your emotions locked up tighter than the Denver Mint.''

''I trusted Hakim.''

''You fell in love with him. Don't hold the arrangement against him, Catherine. The kind of deal we made is pretty common in his part of the world.''

''I figured that out. The fact that I am a means to an end for him doesn't lessen my value in his eyes.''

''Well, as to that, I'm sure you've heard there won't be any need for long-term living visas.''

''What?''

''Didn't Hakim tell you? His uncle's intelligence sprang a trap on the leaders for the dissidents. They're in jail awaiting trial for treason right now.''

Why hadn't Hakim said something? ''When did this happen?''

Looking relieved by the change in topic, her dad said, ''I got word yesterday.''

Yesterday. She remembered the desperation in Hakim's kiss, his mention of sacrifices and there was that initial flash of pain in his eyes when she told him she was pregnant.

She stumbled to her feet. She needed to think. ''I've

got to go.'' She walked quickly toward the door of his office.

"Are you okay?" She hadn't heard her dad get up from his chair, but his hand was on her shoulder.

"I'm fine. Why wouldn't I be?"

"I'm sorry, Catherine. If I could change the way things happened, I would."

She believed him.

Walking into the penthouse fifteen minutes later, she was still trying to make sense of what her father's revelations meant for her and Hakim. She couldn't forget that small flash of pain. What had it meant?

There was no longer any need for long-term living visas. Did he regret their marriage now that the personal benefit to him was gone?

The blinking light on the answering machine caught her attention as she tossed her purse on the table. She couldn't listen to the recording, not yet.

So many thoughts were crowding her mind, she didn't think she could take another one in. Not even a phone message.

She sat down and started dealing with the kaleidoscope of impressions one by one. The foremost was the very first time she and Hakim had shared passion. They hadn't made love, but he'd wanted to, had been aching with the need to have her.

The next image she examined was his reaction to her demand for a divorce. He hadn't just been angry. He'd been furious on a very personal level. And he'd done everything in his power to change her mind. The fact that he'd been successful considering how betrayed she had felt meant something.

Then she thought of her life together with him over

the past weeks. Happy. Content. Pleased with one another's company. Sexually insatiable. In harmony.

They fit together.

She didn't know what that small flash of pain meant, but she was absolutely positive it had not resulted from his discovery he was stuck with her. The fact that he hadn't told her about the capture of the rebels yet indicated that in his mind, that aspect of their marriage was incidental to their relationship.

With that tantalizing thought swirling through her mind, she got up to push the play button on the answering machine.

Hearing the voice of the King of Jawhar was a little unsettling, but hearing his request that she, not Hakim, return his call was enough to make her knees go weak.

CHAPTER THIRTEEN

AFTER taking several deep breaths, she picked up the phone to call the King. Her nervousness only increased when Abdul-Malik insisted on sending her call straight through even though the King was in a meeting.

Their greetings were a little stilted, but it didn't take King Asad long to come to the point. "You have heard the dissidents have been arrested?"

"Yes." She didn't bother to tell him her father, rather than Hakim, had told her the news.

"There is no longer a need for long-term visas."

"I gathered that, yes."

"Another could oversee our business interests abroad. Hakim could come home."

Catherine felt her mouth curve into a smile at the wonderful news and then the King's wording struck her and the smile slipped a little. "Why are you telling me rather than Hakim?"

"I have told my nephew." She could hear the royal impatience clearly across the phone line. "It is my will and the will of his people that he return to rule the Kadar province."

"He didn't mention it." Why hadn't he?

"He refuses to return."

"*What?*" She couldn't believe it. Then she realized she'd just shouted into the ear of a king. "I'm sorry, Your Excellency, but I cannot understand this refusal. My husband wants to return to Jawhar, I know he does."

175

"I am certain of this too, jewel of his heart."

What in the world? Why had he called her that? "Then…"

A heavy sigh and then, "He is convinced you would be unhappy living in Kadar."

"That's ridiculous. I loved our time there. He knows I did."

"I think, perhaps I should tell you a confidence."

She wanted to hear anything that would make sense of this bizarre situation. "Please do."

"It is not something I would share with the wife of my nephew in the usual circumstances, but his stubbornness leaves me no choice."

"I understand," she said with a fair bit of her own impatience.

"Very well. When he was at university, Hakim had a relationship with a woman he believed he loved. A woman he believed loved him."

Maybe Catherine didn't want to hear about this.

"Hakim asked this woman to marry him, to return to Jawhar and live as his sheikha. This was before it was decided he would oversee our business holdings in America."

"She turned him down. He told me."

"She told my nephew that no matter how much she loved him, no western woman would willingly give up her career, her lifestyle and her country to move to a backwater like Kadar." The King's voice dripped acid. "This woman told Hakim he had to choose between his position as a Sheikh of Kadar with life in Jawhar and her."

"He chose his position," Catherine said, stating the obvious. After all, the two had not married.

"But with you, he has found the true jewel of his heart. He chose you over his duty to his people."

"What do you mean?"

"He believes your happiness lies in Seattle, therefore he has refused to return to his homeland and his people."

Catherine's body started shaking and she had to sit down. "But I didn't ask that of him. He never said anything."

"He does not wish to distress you. He told me that he thought you might sacrifice your happiness for his, but he would not allow you to do so."

"But I'd be happier in Kadar. I want to raise our babies in his palace. I like the sunshine. The people are wonderful. I could learn to race camels." She was babbling, but so stunned from the news that Hakim had chosen her over his duty that she couldn't control her tongue.

"Babies?" the King inquired with meaning.

"Oh... I..."

"Perhaps you will have good news to share when you and my nephew return to Jawhar?"

"But Hakim said he doesn't want to come."

"No, Catherine, he said you do not wish to come and therefore he will not."

She bit her lip. What was the King thinking now? "Are you angry with me?"

"No. I spoke to Lila and many whom you had contact with on your visit to Jawhar. I am convinced this problem my nephew believes exists is in his head, not your heart."

"You're right, but what should I do?"

"Tell him your feelings." The King sounded a bit exasperated with her dull thinking.

She smiled. "I want to do more." Hakim deserved a gesture that showed how much she loved him, how much she wanted to live in Jawhar with him. "Maybe you could help me out…"

Hakim opened the door to the penthouse with a sense of anticipation he had never had prior to his marriage. She would be waiting. His Catherine. His little kitten.

Perhaps she would be curled up on the sofa as she had been yesterday. He smiled at the thought. Such a welcome did indeed make up for a lot. It made up for everything. He could live the rest of his life in this damp climate if it meant basking in the warmth of her love.

There would be children. Sooner than later. His heart pounded at the thought. She already carried his child, perhaps a son, the next Sheikh of Kadar. A son who would be an outsider to his people like he had been in the Palace of Jawhar after his parent's death. But the child would belong in their family. He would fit with Catherine and Hakim. It was enough. It had to be enough.

The sound of soft music from the bedroom drew him, but he found the room empty. Eastern music played from the built-in sound system and the door to the lavish en suite bathroom stood open. He walked in to find his wife lounging in the deep sunken bath, the fragrance of jasmine surrounding her, a subtle lure to his senses.

"It would take a man very secure in his masculinity to share his wife's bath when the water has been scented with the oil of fragrant flowers."

Her beautiful head turned, the cupid bow of her mouth tilted in a beguiling smile. "It's lucky for me I'm married to a very macho guy then isn't it?"

His fingers were already at work on the buttons of

his shirt. "It is I who am blessed, my jewel." She glittered like the most precious stone with beauty and fire. "To have such a wife is all any man could ask."

Soft pink colored her cheeks and she averted her eyes. "I never know how to respond when you say stuff like that."

He finished undressing and slipped into the hot water with her. His legs brushed the silken smooth skin of hers. "It is my hope you will accept my words with the flowering of joy in your heart."

She peeked at him through her eyelashes, her expression coquettish, the feel of her foot insinuating itself between his thighs not. "I am very happy with you, Hakim."

And it was true. She radiated with the same glowing joy she had on their wedding day. What had wrought this change? Was it her pregnancy?

Her small, feminine toes caressed his male flesh and he felt an immediate and overwhelming response.

She reached out and brushed the tip of his shaft. "Mmm… Very masculine."

He laughed and launched himself at her.

Later, she snuggled in front of him, her breathing still a little ragged. "I think you drowned me."

"You offered an invitation too appealing to pass up."

"Are you sure it was an invitation? Maybe I was just trying to unwind in a nice, relaxing bath."

He laughed. She often gave him the gift of laughter. "It was a shameless invitation and you know it." He tweaked a still rigid nipple.

She squealed and batted his hand away. "All right. I admit it. Sexy invitation all the way."

"You are that."

"What?" she asked, cuddling more snuggly against him.

"You are incredibly sexy."

"You make me feel like it. You make me feel beautiful." She said it with such surprise.

"Your beauty surpasses that of any other woman."

She sighed and laced her fingers with his across her stomach.

Would she accept his avowal of love now? He had wanted to tell her of his feelings, but although she had admitted she still loved him, she held something back. Her trust. When he told her of his love, he wanted her to believe him, to trust him. If she believed his words of love were insincere, it would hurt her and he could not bear for her to be hurt anymore.

Her kiss surprised him and her lips were gone before he could take advantage of it.

"Your uncle called today."

Tension filled him. "What did he have to say?"

"One of your cousins just got engaged."

This he knew. His uncle had told him that along with the news about the dissidents being captured. "She is not technically my cousin. She is my uncle's niece through his wife."

"He still wants us to come to Jawhar for the betrothal celebration."

His heart ached as it always did when he thought of his home. "Do you wish to go?" They had just gotten back. It was a long journey to take again so soon.

"Oh, yes."

"Then we shall go."

Her smile was all woman and somehow mysterious.

He gave up wondering what it meant when her lips once again covered his own. This time he was ready to take the advantage.

A week later they boarded the same jet that had taken them to Jawhar the first time. Hakim was very attentive on the journey, asking Catherine repeatedly how she felt and if she needed anything. Thankfully, she had experienced only the slightest form of morning sickness with her pregnancy and the flight was no problem at all. Which was a relief considering the plans she had for when they reached the airport.

Hakim led her to the helo pad, believing they were taking a short helicopter ride to his cousin's home province. Catherine kept him occupied with a totally inappropriate display of affection he did not seem to mind in the least and it was an hour before Hakim realized they were headed in the wrong direction.

He tapped the guard seated next to the pilot and yelled something in Arabic. The guard answered and Hakim turned to her, his expression furious.

"What the hell is going on?"

The smug smile she'd meant to greet him with withered in the face of his wrath, but she kept her cool. He couldn't go totally ballistic. After all, being pregnant did have its uses.

"I'm kidnapping you," she shouted above the sound of the helicopter's blades.

His eyes snapped black retribution, but he didn't say another word until they had landed near the Kadar Palace. The same SUV was there to transport them, even the same guards. Catherine smiled at them, trying to ignore the glowering man by her side.

Hakim kept his silence until they had reached the privacy of their bedroom in the palace.

Then he turned to her, menace written in every line of his body. "What is happening?"

"I kidnapped you."

"So you said."

She clasped her hands together in front of her to stop their shaking. This was supposed to be easy. Tell him how she felt about living here, he would be pleased and everything would be fine. Only he was mad, really mad.

"Why are you so angry?"

"You usurp my authority among my people and you have to ask this?"

She hadn't considered that angle. "You have to stop taking yourself so seriously. Your consequence hasn't suddenly taken a nosedive, if that's what you're worried about. As far as everyone else knows, everything has been done according to the will and authority of King Asad. It's no big deal."

Hakim did not look particularly reassured. "And what exactly is this *no big deal*?"

She was getting a little frustrated with his anger. "You had no right to refuse to return to Jawhar without consulting me. I'm your wife, not a mindless bed warmer who has no say in the decisions that affect me. And I'm definitely not that stupid woman you lived with. My thoughts and my feelings are my own. You should have found out what they were before refusing your duty to your family and your country."

She crossed her arms over her chest and glared at him, a little of her own anger coming to the surface as she remembered how he'd made such a major decision without her input.

Hakim rubbed the back of his neck, his expression turning resigned. "My uncle convinced you to sacrifice yourself for me, for the good of my country." It wasn't a question, but she treated it like one anyway.

"No, he did not. He simply told me that you had refused to come home when the capture of the dissidents made it possible."

"We will not be staying." He spun as if to leave the room.

He made her so mad sometimes she wanted to spit. "Hakim!"

He stopped.

"I know you can ride a camel. Heck, you can order a helicopter faster than I can order dinner."

His body tensed. "What is the point of this?"

"I can't hold you here against your will. I can't stop you from leaving by dropping you in a desert encampment from which you have no easy escape."

He turned to face her, his expression not so much unreadable as full of conflicting emotions. "So?"

"I have only one thing to hold you here." If he loved her, it would be enough.

"What?"

"Myself."

He shook his head and she squelched the tiny doubt that tried to intrude on her certainty that he loved her. He had to love her to have chosen her over his duty. A man with his strong sense of responsibility would only make such a decision under a powerful influence of emotion.

"This is not about you." He swung his arm out indicating the room, the palace, Kadar. "This is about my uncle manipulating you into sacrificing your happiness for my duty. I won't allow it."

"How do you know what would make me happy?" she demanded. "You never asked."

"I made a promise to you, to put you first from the point of our marriage forward. I will keep that promise."

"Are you saying it's a promise holding you here in this room with me?"

He stared at her, his expression that of a man trying very hard to hold onto his temper. "I did not say that."

"Good. Am I enough to hold you?" She wanted the words. She deserved the words.

"There is no binding that could be stronger." He started toward her, his intent very clear in the obsidian eyes she loved so much.

Her feet started moving of their own volition, taking her to him. They met in the middle of the room. He pulled her into his arms, his hold so tight she could barely breathe.

"I want to raise my children here," she said breathlessly, "I want them to know the tradition of their father's people, to know the warmth of the desert, the love of a family so big I'll probably never learn everybody's name."

He cupped the back of her nape under her hair. She'd left it down and it was wind-blown from the helicopter ride. "But your job…"

She smiled reassuringly. "I'll expand the library in the palace and make it available to the people."

His groan was that of a man who knew his peaceful existence was in danger of extinction. "There are no cities here, no malls, no movie cinemas—"

She interrupted his litany of Kadar's supposed shortcomings. "I told you I'm not that other woman. I don't like shopping. I don't care for city traffic. I was living in a small town by choice when we met. I love this place. I love the people. How could you not see that when we were here?''

He kissed her and she melted into him. Somehow they ended up on the bed amidst a pile of tasseled pillows.

He leaned above her and brushed the hair from her temple. ''I want you to be happy, *aziz*.''

Her heart constricted with hope and then certainty. ''Because you love me.''

''Of course I love you. Have I not said this a hundred times?''

She could not recall him saying it once. ''No.''

''I have.''

''When?'' she challenged him.

''Do you not know the meaning of *aziz*? I would have thought you would ask my sister or Lila. You had their confidence in every other matter.''

She licked her lips, her heart thrilling when his gaze zeroed in on the movement with feral intent. ''What does it mean?''

''Beloved. Cherished. How could I not love you? You are all that a woman should be, the jewel of my heart.''

Joy suffused her until she was almost sick with it. She grinned. ''When did you realize it?''

Hakim hugged her to him. ''I was pretty stupid. I did not realize these feelings I have for you were love until the day I gave you the telescope and I thought you were still thinking of leaving me. Before that I knew I did not want to let you go, but in that moment, I realized that if you did go, you would take my heart, my soul, with you.''

She started unbuttoning his shirt, wanting to get to

the man beneath. "Why didn't you tell me you loved me then?"

"I was afraid you would not believe me, that my avowal would cause you more pain than pleasure."

She stared at him in disbelief. "How could you think telling me you loved me would hurt me? I was dying inside thinking I was nothing more than a means to an end."

"Forgive me, *aziz*, for my many mistakes, but you are and will always be the ultimate means to my end, for I need you to be happy and without you my life would be as arid as the desert and as empty as a dry well."

The words brought tears to her eyes and finally she knew what to do when he said stuff like that.

Later, their naked limbs entwined on the bed, she smiled at him, her heart a melted puddle of feeling from the many words of love he'd spoken during their love-making. "I love you, Hakim."

He kissed her softly. "I love you, Catherine. It will always be so until the stars fall from the heavens and even beyond."

After a lifetime of not fitting in, she had finally found her place. In his arms. Next to his heart.

It would always be.

The world's bestselling romance series.

HARLEQUIN®
Presents~

Seduction and Passion Guaranteed!

FROM BOARDROOM
TO BEDROOM

**Harlequin Presents® brings you two
original stories guaranteed to make
your Valentine's Day extra special!**

THE BOSS'S
MARRIAGE ARRANGEMENT
by *Penny Jordan*

Pretending to be her boss's mistress is one thing—but now
everyone in the office thinks Harriet is Matthew Cole's
fiancée! Harriet has to keep reminding herself it's all just
for convenience, but how far is Matthew prepared to go
with the arrangement—marriage?

HIS DARLING VALENTINE
by *Carole Mortimer*

It's Valentine's Day, but Tazzy Darling doesn't care.
Until a secret admirer starts bombarding her with gifts!
Any woman would be delighted—but not Tazzy. There's
only one man she wants to be sending her love tokens, and
that's her boss, Ross Valentine. And her secret admirer
couldn't possibly be Ross…could it?

The way to a man's heart…is through the bedroom

The world's bestselling romance series.

Seduction and Passion Guaranteed!

They're the men who have everything—except a bride....

Wealth, power, charm—what else could a heart-stoppingly
handsome tycoon need? In the GREEK TYCOONS
miniseries you have already been introduced to some
gorgeous Greek multimillionaires who are in need of wives.

THE GREEK BOSS'S DEMAND
by *Trish Morey*
On sale January 2005, #2444

THE GREEK TYCOON'S CONVENIENT MISTRESS
by *Lynne Graham*
On sale February 2005, #2445

THE GREEK'S SEVEN-DAY SEDUCTION
by *Susan Stephens*
On sale March 2005, #2455

Pick up a Harlequin Presents® novel and you will enter a world
of spine-tingling passion and provocative, tantalizing romance!

Available wherever Harlequin books are sold.

www.eHarlequin.com

If you enjoyed what you just read,
then we've got an offer you can't resist!

Take 2 bestselling love stories FREE!

Plus get a FREE surprise gift!

Clip this page and mail it to Harlequin Reader Service®

IN U.S.A.	IN CANADA
3010 Walden Ave.	P.O. Box 609
P.O. Box 1867	Fort Erie, Ontario
Buffalo, N.Y. 14240-1867	L2A 5X3

YES! Please send me 2 free Harlequin Presents® novels and my free surprise gift. After receiving them, if I don't wish to receive anymore, I can return the shipping statement marked cancel. If I don't cancel, I will receive 6 brand-new novels every month, before they're available in stores! In the U.S.A., bill me at the bargain price of $3.80 plus 25¢ shipping & handling per book and applicable sales tax, if any*. In Canada, bill me at the bargain price of $4.47 plus 25¢ shipping & handling per book and applicable taxes**. That's the complete price and a savings of at least 10% off the cover prices—what a great deal! I understand that accepting the 2 free books and gift places me under no obligation ever to buy any books. I can always return a shipment and cancel at any time. Even if I never buy another book from Harlequin, the 2 free books and gift are mine to keep forever.

106 HDN DZ7Y
306 HDN DZ7Z

Name	(PLEASE PRINT)	
Address	Apt.#	
City	State/Prov.	Zip/Postal Code

Not valid to current Harlequin Presents® subscribers.

Want to try two free books from another series?
Call 1-800-873-8635 or visit www.morefreebooks.com.

* Terms and prices subject to change without notice. Sales tax applicable in N.Y.
** Canadian residents will be charged applicable provincial taxes and GST.
   All orders subject to approval. Offer limited to one per household.
   ® are registered trademarks owned and used by the trademark owner and or its licensee.

PRES04R   ©2004 Harlequin Enterprises Limited

eHARLEQUIN.com

The Ultimate Destination for Women's Fiction

Calling all aspiring writers!
Learn to craft the perfect romance novel
with our useful tips and tools:

- Take advantage of our **Romance Novel Critique Service** for detailed advice from romance professionals.

- Use our **message boards** to connect with writers, published authors and editors.

- Enter our **Writing Round Robin—** you could be published online!

- Learn many tools of the writer's trade from editors and authors in our **On Writing** section!

- **Writing guidelines** for Harlequin or Silhouette novels—what our editors *really* look for.

The world's bestselling romance series.